Two men dragged Yiska Wilcox down the dirt street, though he put up quite a struggle. He looked back at Eliana, his eyes dark and wild.

"Wait!" she yelled. "He saved me from that wagon!"

"I didn't see no wagon. Did anyone see a wagon?"

"No, all I saw was that stinkin' half blood attack this pretty young lady here." The man grabbed a lock of her hair. Eliana swatted his hand away and stomped on his foot, sending him whimpering away like a wounded coyote.

"What is the meaning of this?" Her father shouted. The men backed away from Eliana. Others peered out from storefronts.

"Papa!" Eliana ran to her father's side.

"Daughter, what happened?" Eliana clung to him. "What's going on here?" he called over her. Eliana shifted behind her father, still holding his arm.

"Don't worry, mister. We hauled that half-breed varmint off to the jail."

CARLA OLSON GADE has been imagining stories for most of her life. Her love for writing and eras gone by turned her attention to writing historical Christian romance. She is a member of American Christian Fiction Writers and Maine Fellowship of Christian Writers. An autodidact, creative thinker, and avid reader, Carla also enjoys genealogy, web design, and photography. A native New Englander, she writes from her home in beautiful rural Maine where she resides with her "hero" husband and two young adult sons. You may visit her online at www.carlagade.com.

The Shadow Catcher's Daughter

Carla Olson Gade

Heartsong Presents

For those who seek the love of the heavenly Father.

*In memory of my stepfather, Ronald Buckley,
my wild west consultant, who during the writing
of this book took his own journey heavenward.*

A note from the Author:
*I love to hear from my readers! You may correspond with me by
writing:*

**Carla Olson Gade
Author Relations
P.O. Box 9048
Buffalo, NY 14240-9048**

ISBN-13: 978-0-373-48602-1

THE SHADOW CATCHER'S DAUGHTER

This edition issued by special arrangement with Barbour Publishing, Inc.,
1810 Barbour Drive, Uhrichsville, Ohio, U.S.A.

one

May, 1875
Del Norte, Colorado Territory

"Imagine having to bear a mark like that for the rest of your life." Eliana Van Horn thrust the *San Juan Prospector* into her father's face as they ambled down the boardwalk of the thriving supply town at the base of the San Juan Mountains. "The tattoo on her chin, how dreadful—and there's nothing that can be done about it!"

John Van Horn peered at the picture from beneath his spectacles. "Yes, Olive Oatman, the Indian captive." He drew his mouth into a tight line and stroked his graying beard. "Everyone has some kind of mark."

Eliana held her head high against the Colorado mountains. "Yes, I know." *All too well.*

Her father loosened his tie, which seemed to be constricting his neck, and cleared his throat. "You've seen that engraving before. That photograph has been in circulation for nearly a decade. Amazing that she's still in the public interest after all this time."

"The article says that the editor of her captivity narrative has died. Apparently, through the years, her husband bought and destroyed every available copy of *The Captivity of the Oatman Girls*. She no longer lectures and wears a veil to cover her tattoo when in public."

"Yet, her picture will continue to tell the story even if the

5

books are gone. Photography does create a permanent record, for good or gain," Papa said.

Eliana pulled the newspaper back and curled it around her chin. Was it right to perpetuate this woman's shame, wrought by the natives? Photography had its merits, but should it have limits as well? And what about the indelible mark etched on her soul? As for the book, Eliana still possessed her own copy and had been intrigued by the tale for years. Utmost, that despite the atrocities Olive suffered at the hands of her captors, she saw God's hand of mercy when she was kept from starvation by a kind Indian woman. It was then that Olive learned to chide her hasty judgment against all the Indian race.

Eliana also hoped to keep from making hasty judgments. She knew for some, it was enough to be judged simply for the color of their skin. Dare she liken it to the prejudice she received as a woman? Some people wanted to make their mark on the world, while others could never hide from the marks they received. But at what cost?

What would it be like to be attacked or captured by Indians? A shiver crawled up her spine as Eliana studied the picture while she and her father walked along. As her father's photography assistant, Eliana was always fascinated by images in print. And she'd much rather discuss photography than Indians. "If I were her, I'd get a new tintype done and have it retouched to make that terrible mark disappear," she said.

"As for retouching, my photography mentor in Ohio is renowned for that process. You know. . ." Papa stopped dead in his tracks and caught Eliana by the elbow. "You're not worried, Sunshine, are you? If you're hesitant about going on the expedition, now is the time to say so."

Images whirled around Eliana's vivid imagination like a zoetrope as she recalled hearing about the attack on the Slack ranch last year. The Utes burned the new resident out and almost started an Indian war right in the San Juans. Eliana peered at the mountain vista and wondered where renegade

Indians hid. She and Papa would travel through wild country soon on their assignment for the U.S. General Land Office. She drew in a deep breath of the fresh Colorado air to cleanse her mind from the unwelcome thoughts that had spun into her head.

"I have no reservations whatsoever. We've made many preparations for this trip, and I won't abandon you. It's too important. This is your big chance." *And mine.* "You've already assured me that this is one of the safest times to go." She tilted her head. "Besides, I'm not afraid of—"

"No Injuns allowed!" A voice bellowed from inside the Silver Eagle Saloon. Head over boots, some unfortunate soul tumbled through the swinging doors, whirring past the Van Horns like a windstorm. Eliana's newspaper flew into the dusty street.

Papa steadied and reached out for her. "Are you all right, dear?"

Eliana gasped as she clung to the porch post and attempted to regain her composure. "I'm fine." At least she was until an oversized man stepped out onto the planking, nearly knocking her over again.

" 'Scuse me, miss." The stench of saloon and neglected ablutions clung to him. "Just doin' a little housekeepin'. Don't want no half breeds stinkin' up the place. The owner ain't partial to his kind." He spit into the road, muttered an oath, and tromped back inside.

&

Yiska Wilcox sprang to his feet. He brushed the dirt from his pants and the pebbles from his calloused hands. He'd been kicked out of places like this before and swore he'd never go in again. A lungful of exasperation escaped his clenched teeth. Things never changed.

A young woman stared at him like a stunned doe. A middle-aged man stood beside her, a protective grip around her waist. He took in the pair with a furtive scan. The man wore a linen duster over his suit and a bowler hat. Assayer maybe. Surveyor possibly. Or maybe another easterner out to make a fortune. As for his companion, she was a lady if he ever saw one—a rare occurrence in his travels. Even in that pretty dress, she carried no highfalutin airs. A natural beauty.

"Beg your pardon, sir, miss. I hope you aren't harmed."

"Not at all." The man surveyed Yiska head to toe. "Are we, dear?"

"We're quite fine, thank you," the young lady said, her bright eyes scrutinizing him.

"Are you all right, young man? You're the one who was tossed out on his ear." The gentleman stooped to pick up the pipe he had dropped.

"Yes, sir." Yiska flicked his hair away from his face and dragged his fingers through his hair. Where'd his hat go? A brisk wind blew a sheet of newsprint toward him, and it clung to his legs like buffalo bur.

"Now, if you'd be so kind as to hand me my newspaper, I'd appreciate it very much," the lady said.

Yiska grasped the paper and spotted the image of the famous Indian captive, Olive Oatman—the chin tattoo the telling sign. Seemed folks never grew weary of recounting the tale. They even wrote dime novels about her. But the sad truth was that the southwest tribe, Apache they claimed, had abducted her and her sister in their youth from a westbound wagon in Arizona and later sold them to the Mohave. He didn't claim to understand such things, though something akin to regret twinged his heart. At least she was eventually ransomed.

The young woman extended her ivory hand, cuffed in a ruffle of lace that poked out from her jacket sleeve. Her eyes met his directly—the color of sagebrush, with a mixture of mystery and curiosity. He handed her the newspaper. When their fingertips touched, she quickly drew the paper into her protective custody. She acknowledged Yiska with a nod and stepped back. Had she felt the tremor, too? Probably just scared—of him.

Yiska tried not to stare at the marks on the young lady's chin. Must be newspaper ink. The man tapped his forefinger against his own chin, handed her a handkerchief, and said in a low voice, "Dear, you've some ink on your chin." Her eyes darted toward Yiska and back again in alarm. And then her face became as red as a Colorado sunset. Obviously mortified, she turned her pretty head, facing the saloon. Men leered from the uncurtained windows, and she spun back around. Yiska scowled at the scoundrels. What was this woman doing out in front of a saloon in the first place?

After her discreet attempt to wipe her face, she glanced up from beneath her dark lashes with a smirk. "I guess you can't take me anywhere, can you, Papa?" Yiska noticed the slight dimple in her adorable chin.

Her father chuckled then sobered. "I certainly never should've let you cross the street with me." The gentleman's eyes shot toward Yiska. He rocked up on his toes, hands deep in his pockets. "Why don't you tell me what happened in there?"

"I went in to get my wages. Wasn't planning to stay. I'm not overly welcome in such fine establishments." Yiska knew there was a defensive edge to his voice. Did it matter anymore?

"Haven't seen you around here before," the man said, "but then we're fairly new to these parts." Yiska hadn't seen them either. The mining supply town had folks coming and going all the time, especially now that the snow was gone.

"I just rode in." Yiska glanced at his borrowed mount tied to the hitching post. "I came to claim my pay from my boss. I was told I'd find him here."

"Looks like you'll have to wait until he comes out."

"He ain't coming out. Not before my silver's all gone." Yiska kicked the dirt.

The man's eyes narrowed. "What's your boss's name?"

"Trask Whiley, the outfitter. I'm one of his guides. Been out on the trail."

"I know him. He's been helping us get settled in the region." The man glanced at the saloon door. "I'll tell you what. I'll go in and talk to him for you. I've some business of my own to discuss with him. You'll have to stay out here, Eliana."

"Surely, Papa. You didn't think I wanted to go in there with you?"

"They might toss you out on your ear, too," Yiska said.

"Ah, the life of a second-rate citizen."

At that, Yiska cocked his head and raised an eyebrow.

Her cheeks reddened. "I was referring to myself, a female. I didn't mean to imply. . ."

Her father cleared his throat. "What's your name, son?"

"Yiska. Yiska Wilcox." He held out his hand. The man shook it with a firm grip.

"John Van Horn. And this is my lovely daughter, Eliana Van Horn."

"Mr. Van Horn." Yiska nodded. "Miss Van Horn."

"Mr. Wilcox, I'd be obliged if you would see my daughter safely across Main Street and wait for me right there in front of Gray's Mercantile. I'll be out in two shakes of a lamb's tail."

The man was confident. His daughter—endearing.

"That's mighty generous of you, Mr. Van Horn." Yiska nodded. "And I'd be happy to see to your daughter's safety."

"How much pay do you have coming to you?" Van Horn asked.

"Twenty-six dollars, sir. . .and a new hat."

"I'll see what I can do. You said your name's Wilcox?"

"Yes, sir. Yiska Wilcox. He knows me well."

"Wilcox. . ." Van Horn shook his head and chuckled. "That's a good old English name."

❧

"Miss Van Horn, shall we?"

Eliana thought Mr. Wilcox was about to offer her his arm, but he kept a respectful distance. They walked across Del Norte's main street—she in her new dress and reticule, and he in a buckskin vest with a tomahawk strapped to his hip. Tumbleweeds rolled in her stomach. What was her father thinking? She had never met an Indian before, never mind walked across the street with one. To her surprise he was relatively polite, though a little rough around the edges. Certainly not what she expected. She did have expectations, after all.

"How long do you suppose two shakes of a lamb's tail takes, Miss Van Horn?" His grin revealed a nice smile, which added to his rather handsome facial features—high cheekbones, broad forehead, strong jaw, dark almond eyes. Not that she noticed.

Eliana laughed. So, he had a sense of humor. "I don't know, probably about the same as two crows of a rooster. Or three moos of a cow."

"Or four screams of a hawk," he chimed in.

"Good one!" Oh, dear. She hoped he wouldn't misconstrue her amusement for flirting. Eliana hastened her stride.

The ground beneath them rumbled. A wagon barreled around the corner, drawn by a team of wild-eyed horses. Dust kicked up in a cloud. Mr. Wilcox shoved Eliana to one side and almost landed on top of her. Their fall nearly knocked the wind from her lungs. She swiped the dust from her lips and groaned.

"Miss Van Horn?" Mr. Wilcox spoke in a concerned tone and gently placed his hand upon her back. "Miss Van Horn, are you all right?"

"Yes, I believe so. . . ."

Some men gathered round, and one yanked Mr. Wilcox up by the shirt. Another punched him in the stomach. Mr. Wilcox doubled over.

Another man pulled Eliana up by both arms, right into his chest. She jumped back. She didn't know whether to thank the man or slap him.

Two men dragged Yiska Wilcox down the dirt street, though he put up quite a struggle. He looked back at Eliana, his eyes dark and wild.

"Wait!" she yelled. "He saved me from that wagon!"

"I didn't see no wagon. Did anyone see a wagon?"

"No, all I saw was that stinkin' half blood attack this pretty young lady here." The man grabbed a lock of her hair. Eliana swatted his hand and stomped on his foot, sending him whimpering away like a wounded coyote.

"What is the meaning of this?" Her father shouted. The men backed away from Eliana. Others peered out from storefronts.

"Papa!" Eliana ran to her father's side.

"Daughter, what happened?" Eliana clung to him. "What's going on here?" he called over her. Eliana shifted behind her father, still holding his arm.

"Don't worry, mister. We hauled that half-breed varmint off to the jail."

"I wasn't aware this town had a jail," Papa said.

One of the men in the crowd smiled at Eliana, exposing several missing teeth. "We're always looking out for the ladies in this town. Yes, siree."

"Ladies?" Someone snickered beneath his breath.

Eliana tugged on his sleeve, "Papa, we must do something!"

"What's all the commotion about, Van Horn?" A familiar voice penetrated the crowd. Trask Whiley. Mr. Whiley held a certain measure of respect from most of the town folk, and he didn't appear to be inebriated. "Get outta here! Git!"

The men went off in various directions, but most of them disappeared inside the Silver Eagle Saloon.

"Now, Eliana, why don't you tell us exactly what happened?" her father asked.

"Mr. Wilcox was escorting me across the street to the mercantile, as you requested, when a wagon came tearing around the corner. If it hadn't been for Mr. Wilcox. . . He saved my life!"

"Where'd they take him, John?"

"To the jail, they said."

Mr. Whiley seemed to note the question in her father's eyes.

"They mean Thatcher's Sawmill."

A dreadful foreboding gripped Eliana. "What will they do to him?"

"We'd better get right over there." Whiley said. "It's their word against his. And I'm afraid it doesn't take much of an excuse to hang an Injun."

two

"There are only two reasons a wagon would drive that fast through this little town—one is Indians, and the other is gold," Trask Whiley explained as he drove Eliana and her father toward Thatcher's Sawmill.

Eliana gripped the edge of the seat. Would they get there in time to rescue Yiska Wilcox from certain execution?

"I thought silver was the main commodity in the San Juans," Papa said. "And what of the Indians? There haven't been reports of danger around here lately." He remained calm and collected, but Eliana could tell he was agitated by the way he gnawed on the end of his unlit pipe.

"Precisely," Whiley said. "Silver's aplenty, so when someone finds gold there's a big hullabaloo. As for Indians, the townsfolk think they've got themselves one now."

"He's not full-blooded," Eliana said.

"No matter. His blood's considered tainted by most."

"That's barbaric!" Eliana wrung her hands and frowned. How could the kind act of a stranger turn into such a fiasco? *Dear Lord, please let us get to him in time. Oh, please!*

"It's what some call Western justice, Miss Van Horn." Whiley snapped the reins.

"There's no justice in this at all," her father said. "The man was protecting my daughter!"

Whiley pulled up in front of the San Luis Valley Bank. An old wagon loaded with shovels, pickaxes, and all kinds of miscellany sat parked in front with a pair of lathered horses hitched to the rig. "Stay put. When I come out of there I should have the proof we need to verify your story, Miss Van Horn."

"Then will they let Mr. Wilcox go?"

"That remains to be seen." Trask Whiley jumped off his buckboard and marched into the bank.

Eliana tapped her foot against the wagon floor. Mr. Whiley told them that Yiska Wilcox was one of his best employees. Mr. Wilcox worked as a guide all around the Colorado Territory's southwest. As a Navajo he had great instincts, and as a white, he was more trusted. Obviously that didn't always hold true.

❧

Two men hauled Yiska in the direction of Thatcher's Sawmill, home to the town's temporary jail. His hands were tied behind his back with a rough cord. As they passed a huge saw blade, one of the men slammed Yiska down on the table, putting his head within inches of the moving guillotine—a mock execution. The buzzing noise was deafening, but his heart thundered louder still.

"Get that man off of there!" yelled Ed Thatcher.

The hooligan pulled Yiska to his feet. "You have yerself a prisoner, Thatcher."

"This Injun tried to kill a gal downtown," the other fellow said.

Yiska stood up straight, his face set like flint.

"Is that true?" Thatcher booted Yiska in the shin. "Is that true, I said!"

Yiska gritted his teeth, not giving way to the pain.

One of the other men yanked Yiska back by the hair.

"She was about to get run over, so I pushed her out of the way."

"I see. A real hero, are we?"

"I ain't never seen an Injun who was a hero before." The man tightened his hold, straining Yiska's shoulders back.

"He ain't no real Injun. He's a half blood. Them's worse," the other man said.

"What, did your Injun papa have his way with a white woman? The way I see it, you're following in his savage ways," the one holding him taunted.

The muscles in Yiska's jaw tightened, his eyes an icy glare.

"Here's his tomahawk." His captor handed it to Ed Thatcher. "I wanted to keep it fer myself, but it's evidence. Thought there'd be some feathers and stuff on it. It's pretty ordinary if ya ask me."

"It's a hatchet, you imbecile. He used this on the woman?" Thatcher asked.

"Some were sayin'."

"Take him back to the pit!"

The so-called jail was an old storage room filled with grimy buckets and sacks of grain for the mill's pack animals. As the men dragged Yiska into the cell, a rat scurried off. The brutes held him down while Thatcher secured shackles to Yiska's ankles.

"You can't keep me here. I broke no law," Yiska managed through his clenched teeth.

"We'll let the marshal in Colorado Springs decide about that. He oughtta be coming by a few months down the road. After we notify him, of course."

"If'n we notify 'im," one of them scoffed.

Yiska scrambled back as the ruffians came at him with hardwood planks.

"Go on! You've done your job!" Thatcher threw his hand up and halted them, but not before one of them hit Yiska in the side.

Thatcher closed the door to the pen, locked it, and left Yiska in misery.

❧

Bewildered, Yiksa tried to focus in the dim cell. He rustled his boots in the dirty sawdust, a foul odor assailing him. How'd he end up in this lousy mess? After he rode into town on that ornery loaned mount, he'd learned that Mr. Whiley was down at the saloon, probably frivoling away Yiska's month's wages—buying a little time until he came in from the range. Whiley always promised he'd take good care of Yiska. Said when he gambled Yiska's wages, it was an investment on his behalf—truth being that Whiley didn't always come out ahead. His boss had a lot of sense, except when it came to cards and women. But unlike Whiley, Yiska wasn't one to take a risk.

Of course when he entered the Silver Eagle, he'd got tossed out again on his backside. Didn't it figure that Miss Van Horn—Eliana—had to witness the whole thing? The pretty lady and her father seemed like fine people, not prejudiced like others—a rare thing in these parts. Why couldn't folks see that he was no different from anyone else? He loved the Colorado wilderness, he worked hard, and he appreciated the beauty of a lovely woman like Eliana Van Horn. What was he thinking? He'd never stand a chance with someone like her. Nor did his lifestyle as a wilderness guide give him an opportunity to ever be with anyone. Period. The path he took was a lonely one.

Yiska sighed. But wasn't she somethin'? That Eliana Van Horn looked like an angel that dropped right out of heaven, plumb into the Colorado Territory! She was all sunlight on this cloudy Colorado morning. She looked all fancy and feminine in her bustled dress and matching hat, but he reckoned there was more about her than met the eye. Something radiated from her like a jolt of lightning, striking a connection between them.

Yiska sat on the floor and rested his head against his knees. A few streaks of light made their way through the crevices of the outside wall and fell upon his shoulders. Should he pray to the Great Spirit in his distress, or the Christian God? Whoever would listen.

"I could use a little help here. Please set me free," he whispered. If the gods chose to answer his prayer, he had no doubt in his heart that Miss Eliana Van Horn, her father, and Trask Whiley would be along soon. He wanted to believe that Miss Van Horn was different. She wouldn't lie about what had happened, would she?

&

"He's taking a long time, Eliana. I'm going in to see what's holding them up." Eliana's father jumped down from the buckboard. "Will you be all right here for a moment?"

"Yes, Papa, I'll be fine." Eliana shaded her eyes with her hand and returned a wave to a woman sweeping the boardwalk in the distance. "If anyone bothers me again, I'm sure Mrs. Sanborn will notice and send some help."

Her father chuckled. "You're right about that." Mrs. Sanborn never missed a thing. She probably knew all about this afternoon's incident near the saloon and certainly helped usher the news all over town by sharing it with the patrons of her café.

"Please make haste, Papa. Mr. Wilcox's life may be at stake." As her father walked up the steps of the bank, Eliana heard a hawk scream. *Four screams of a hawk.* Oh, Yiska. Before it screamed again she climbed down from the wagon and scooted into the bank after Papa.

They approached the assayer's barred window, where Mr. Whiley hovered over an old man—the miner—who could clear this matter up.

Mr. Whiley thumped his fingers on the counter and looked up at them. "He refused to leave until his gold was counted." So, the man *had* found gold.

"And I promised him a photograph," Whiley added.

"Now?" Eliana and Papa said in unison.

"No. At his claim, after all this is settled."

The miner looked their way with a toothless grin stretching from ear to ear.

"That was the only way I could get him to hurry it up and come with us."

"Very well," Papa said. "If he cooperates I'll even frame the photograph. Where's your claim, mister?"

"I cain't go telling you that until it's registered," the miner said.

Papa shook his head. For years he'd been photographing Colorado mining activities for the U.S. General Land Office. Thousands of ravenous miners and prospectors flooded the mountains and rivers. At one point Papa had even talked to Eliana about staking a claim himself. He wanted to have enough money to send her back East to Ohio to attend finishing school.

"Papa, you have a treasure trove already right there in your camera," she'd said. "And everything I want to know comes from you." He'd always been a good provider, and she wanted to learn all she could from him about photography.

❧

At last the claim was filed. The old miner checked on his horses, paid a boy to bring his rig to the livery, and climbed aboard Mr. Whiley's buckboard. He wore a threadbare shirt and a pair of grimy overalls patched up with old flour sacks. Eliana couldn't help but notice the one that covered his rear with the company's stamp, XXXX. She flattened her lips to stifle a nervous giggle.

Trask Whiley snapped the reins and raced for the mill at the end of town. Eliana covered her face with her hands to keep the dust out of her mouth.

"Howdy, miss." The miner peered at her with a wrinkled grin. "I understand an apology's in order. Didn't see anyone in the road when I came 'round the corner of Main Street. Course, I was going so fast, if I'd blinked I'd missed ya anyway." The unkempt man reeked. Like many others, he'd probably not bathed in at least six months.

Had he just apologized? Eliana thought not.

"Well, Mr. . . ." The wagon hit a bump and jostled her closer to him.

"Cornelius Crawford's the name."

"Mr. Crawford, thank you for agreeing to set matters straight. It would be a shame to have an innocent man pay for a crime he did not commit."

"Wouldn't want anybody to suffer unnecessarily." The corners of the man's weather-beaten face turned downward, making him resemble an old mule. They rode on in silence. A moment later Crawford leaned close to Eliana with a big grin. "Did ya know I'm rich? I'm rich! Now I can find me a wife."

Eliana jumped back. She couldn't get to the sawmill fast enough.

"Whoa!" Mr. Whiley brought his team to a halt.

❧

Eliana, her father, Mr. Whiley, and Mr. Crawford all hustled past the piles of lumber and buzzing saw blades, the scent of fresh-cut aspen filling the air. When they got to the overseer's office, Mr. Thatcher greeted them. "Something I can do for you folks?"

"Where is he?" Whiley demanded.

"I take it you mean the prisoner," Thatcher said. "Don't worry, he's all tied up. Can't hurt anyone where he is."

"Tied up?" Eliana cried. Her father placed his arm around her. She glanced about. In what sort of makeshift jail were they keeping him?

Whiley leaned close to Thatcher's face. "Let me see him. He's my employee—I have a right. And these folks are coming, too."

"Very well. I'm just holding him here until I get the say so."

"Say so?" What did he mean by that? Eliana blinked back the tears forming in her eyes.

They entered a small caged room at the rear of the large building. Mr. Wilcox sat on the floor in the corner, leaning back against the wall, head hung low. His ankles were chained together and attached to a large iron ring on the wall. Heavy ropes bound his wrists.

"Yiska!" Whiley called to him.

Yiska looked up with a great measure of relief and climbed to his feet.

"We got here as soon as we could," Papa said.

Crawford took a step closer and squinted. "I thought you said he was innocent. Why, he's an Injun! Let him rot in there." He turned and started to leave.

Eliana went after him, hands on her hips. "Mr. Crawford!

You can't mean that!"

"Ev-er-y word. I've got my principles."

"Please. . . You must tell the truth—that you came around the corner in your wagon."

"Already told you, I didn't see anyone."

Eliana's father stepped forward. "But you did drive your wagon in haste down Main Street."

"Mr. Crawford, you tell the truth now, or I'll. . ." Oh, how tempting it would be to grab that piece of lumber over there and whack him right across the Xs! Eliana let out a deep breath and softened her voice. "Since you are such a dear, hard-working, and honorable man, I know that you would never want harm to come to anyone. Please tell Mr. Thatcher the truth and let this matter be done. Then you can go back to your gold claim."

Whiley pressed in, glowering at him.

"All right!" Crawford threw his hands in the air. "Yes, I drove my wagon down Main Street on the way to the bank." He looked at Thatcher. "The girl said I near plowed her down. Didn't see her."

"Thank you ever so much, Mr. Crawford." She feigned a smile Papa winked at her, nodding for her to continue. "Mr. Thatcher, Mr. Wilcox saw that wagon coming and was brave enough to push me out of harm's way. When some bystanders saw that we had fallen to the ground, they made a very wrong assumption about Mr. Wilcox. I owe him my life, and he does not deserve to be punished. Now, if you would be so kind as to release this man. . ."

"Yes, ma'am. Grover, get me those keys." Eliana recognized the other man as one who had brought Mr. Wilcox here. Thatcher took the keys and freed Mr. Wilcox from his bonds.

&

Yiska rubbed his wrists as he stepped out of the crude prison. He met everyone's gazes and rested his eyes on the prettiest of all. "Thank you." If he could, he would devote his life to protect them—protect *her*—from any danger. Until then, words alone would have to convey his gratitude. Yiska raked a hand through his hair and exhaled. He clamped his mouth shut as pain shot through his side. They'd confiscated his hatchet and exchanged it for what felt like a broken rib.

"It is I who should thank you. You protected my daughter, and that means everything to me." Mr. Van Horn offered Yiska a firm handshake.

"Well done, Yiska," his boss said.

Mr. Van Horn reached into his pocket. "That reminds me, I have your wages." He handed him some paper notes and several coins. "I put a little extra in there for you."

"That's not necessary, Mr. Van Horn." Yiska glanced at Miss Van Horn. He would do it all again if he had to.

"Please take it. This has caused you a lot of trouble."

Thatcher handed Yiska his hatchet. "I believe this belongs to you."

Yiska walked through the door without turning back.

Outside Whiley placed his hand on Yiska's shoulder. "How about we all go get something to eat?"

"Me, too?" Crawford asked.

"We're just going to Sanborn's Café for a quick bite," Whiley said. "Since you're a rich man now, you ought to go clean up and take yourself out to a proper restaurant. We'll drop you off at the livery, and you can be on your way."

Cornelius Crawford straightened his shoulders. "I think I will." He turned to Miss Van Horn and wiggled his eyebrows. "Care to join me?"

three

Relief washed over Yiska when they finally dropped Crawford off at the livery. Although he was grateful that the man had finally fessed up, Yiska didn't like the way he ogled Miss Van Horn and bragged about his new-found wealth.

As they drove away, the old miner waved his floppy hat in the air and hollered, "What about my daguerreotype? You promised!" Eliana, her father, and Mr. Whiley burst into laughter. Yiska shrugged his shoulders and enjoyed Miss Van Horn's wide smile and dancing eyes.

Whiley parked his rig near Sanborn's Café. Yiska reached up and took Miss Van Horn by the waist to help her down. Her eyes stayed hitched on his while he lowered her to the ground. He winced in pain, but with her looking at him, he soon forgot about it. As he set her down, he hesitated before he let her go.

"Oh, Mr. Wilcox." Her hands remained steadied against his arms, her voice barely above a whisper. "I feel so responsible. Can you ever forgive me?"

"There's nothing to forgive, Miss Van Horn."

"Are you injured?" She took a step back, looking him over, and her cheeks colored.

He hooked his thumbs in his pants pockets. "Only my pride." He held his gaze but wanted to take in *all* of her, from the tousled honey locks peeking out from her hat to her tiny laced boots.

Miss Van Horn glanced at the ground then looked at him beneath dark lashes. In the silence of the moment somehow their hearts spoke, yet there remained a quiet resistance.

"Injun, Injun, stinking Injun!" some mischievous boys shouted out. The rascals disappeared between some buildings.

Eliana shrank back, the spell broken. Her eyes shot to

23

Yiska's hatchet. She said nothing.

"Mr. Wilcox," her father called. He tossed Yiska his hat.

Yiska caught it with both hands.

"Hey, you found it! Mighty obliged, Mr. Van Horn." He dipped his head and put the hat in its rightful place.

As they approached Sanborn's Café, Mr. Whiley held open the door, allowing Miss Van Horn to enter, and then slipped in behind her. He handed off the door to Yiska with a triumphant grin. What was Whiley up to now?

❧

As the troupe entered the café, customers murmured and gave them odd looks. Mrs. Sanborn scurried over and greeted them with all measure of curiosity. "Eliana, dear. I'm glad to see you're doing well. I heard you had quite a time of it today. Almost got run over by a herd of wild horses, and then attacked by an Indian." Mrs. Sanborn eyed Yiska. It was obvious she wondered where *he* fit in to all of this.

Eliana laughed. "I was almost run over by a wagon, but *this* gentleman saved my life." She hoped that would set things straight. What was it like to have to live under a veil of judgement?

Mrs. Sanborn looked at Yiska with astonishment. "Is that so?" Not waiting for a response, she rattled off the day's menu and took their orders.

The pleasing aroma of Mrs. Sanborn's famous pot roast and strawberry rhubarb pie filled the air. She brought their meals to the table herself, serving Yiska last.

"We've much to be thankful for this day," Eliana's father declared. He reached for her hand and lowered his head in silent prayer. Eliana bowed but dared not close her eyes for fear that her emotions of the day would catch up with her. When she peeked up she saw Mr. Whiley busy cutting his meat, but Yiska remained still until her father was done and had tucked his napkin into his vest.

"Do you think we'll see more of Cornelius Crawford?" Mr. Whiley asked with a chortle.

"I believe I'll have to. I've an appointment to keep with him," Papa answered.

"John, you don't mean you'll actually follow through with it?"

"I'm a man of my word, Trask. It was part of the bargain." Papa leaned back in his chair and looked at Yiska. "As a matter of fact, I hope you'll allow me to take your photograph as a small token of my appreciation."

"Photograph? That's what you were laughing about."

Eliana said, "Yes, poor Mr. Crawford called it a daguerreo-type. They haven't been used in ages!"

"You're a photographer." Yiska eyed Papa curiously.

"Yes, and Eliana is my able assistant. We have a temporary studio rented on Alpine Street while we're in town."

"Been here long, sir?"

"Not long enough. We were stuck up at our residence in Lake City all winter and had to wait until the thaw to come down for supplies. It's been good work here since the San Juan Secession of '73 opened up the mining again. And now it's safe for folks to settle here with no real threat of Indians."

Eliana almost spilled her appleade. The table grew quiet.

Yiska shifted in his chair. Had Papa offended him? "Well... you never know what kind of trouble they'll cause. Probably twice as much trouble as I would." He cracked a smile and glanced Eliana's way.

The men all laughed, and the awkward moment faded away. But Eliana remained quiet. How often must Mr. Wilcox deflect comments like that? Did they hurt his feelings? Could someone like him ever fit in with her circle of friends?

Mr. Whiley stood and patted his belly. "I've got a card game to go finish. John, want to play a hand?"

"You know I'm not a gambling man, Whiley. Besides, I think I've had enough excitement for one day. Don't you agree, Sunshine?"

"Indeed, Papa." Eliana sighed. "You are all heroes, and again I thank you."

"I think you are forgetting someone, dear."

"Am I?" What was Papa going to say now?

"Yes, Miss Van Horn. *You* saved my life," Mr. Wilcox said.

Eliana felt her cheeks warm. Papa put his hand on Mr. Wilcox's shoulder and shook his hand. "Yiska, be sure to come over to my studio someday before you head back out. I won't take no for an answer."

"Miss Van Horn, a pleasure as always." Mr. Whiley cocked his head and grinned.

"Likewise," said Mr. Wilcox with a nod.

As she watched him leave, she sincerely hoped he would come by for the photograph. If he didn't, she might never see him again. And that would be a tragedy.

❧

Eliana settled into her bed that night in the Van Horns' apartment above the photography shop. After reading a passage from her Bible, she placed it back on the nightstand, distracted by thoughts from earlier in the day. For a fleeting moment she had thought, had wished, Mr. Wilcox would kiss her when he helped her off the wagon. What was she thinking? It had been broad daylight, in the middle of town. She barely knew the man, yet her heart sensed a familiarity, a longing. Her attraction to him surprised her. His strong face and dark eyes held warmth and interest, the contours around his mouth revealed character, and his thick, shoulder-length brown hair and russet skin tone told of his heritage. All of it reminded her that they were worlds apart, he an Indian, and she. . .

Eliana turned the wick of the oil lamp back and snuggled the counterpane under her chin. She tossed about, trying to get comfortable. Although she was exhausted, she still couldn't sleep. What began as a simple morning of running errands with her father turned into. . . And then it hit her. She could have died or been seriously injured today. The tears began to flow as she pressed her face into her pillow.

"Thank You, Lord, for protecting me and saving my life," she whispered. "Thank You for sending Mr. Wilcox to be there at the right time. Please bless him." More tears flowed. What if he had died, too, this day? Eliana was certain she would join her mother in heaven. But Mr. Wilcox—what did he believe about the afterlife? More importantly, would he inherit eternal life with Christ Jesus? She would never know unless she saw him again. *Lord, please allow me to see Mr. Wilcox again, to share Your love with him. And if it is Your will. . .* No, *that* she dare not ask.

❧

Yiska moaned as he stood from the bunk in a back room at Whiley's Outfitters and stretched. He hadn't wanted to complain in front of the Van Horns, especially Eliana. They already felt bad enough. Fact was, his captors had roughed him up pretty good. Bruised ribs, black and blue shins, and he ached all over like he'd been trampled by a herd of stampeding buffalo.

After the jail incident three days ago—or had it been four—he'd gone to check on his borrowed horse to discover the old mare had been taken over to the livery. There he found his saddle, blanket, and the rest of his stuff heaped in a pile in the corner of a stall. His saddlebag had been ransacked, but the thief hadn't taken everything. Must have been scared off. Now he'd have to replace some supplies and clothing—all of which he could get from Whiley's store. But his small blanket had disappeared—along with the journal he had wrapped inside. That could never be replaced. His sole companion on the trail other than his faithful horse, it was filled with pages describing the Colorado territory's wondrous landscapes. Yiska wrote what he saw and in his own way mined the beauty of the San Juans without destroying any bit of it. He hoped someday to share the riches he wrote about—the snow-capped mountains, brilliant vistas, valleys teeming with wildlife—with those who might never get to enjoy them firsthand. To him it was worth more than gold. And now it was gone.

Yiska had searched around town, hoping his journal might turn up somewhere. It wouldn't have value to anyone but himself. Maybe he'd find that someone had tossed it away. So he looked around behind an old building near the Silver Eagle, and Grover and one of his buddies attacked him. One held him and the other whacked him in the ribs. The pain pierced his side, and Yiska felt like he would pass out. If a rib or two weren't broken before, they surely were now.

But a surge of adrenaline came from nowhere, and he pushed back with what strength he had and kicked Grover into a pile of rubbish. Yiska turned and knocked his other assailant senseless. He managed to make it back to Mr. Whiley, who had tended his bruises. Now he finally felt like getting up.

He walked over to the washbowl and splashed water on his face. After he shaved, he grabbed the fresh shirt, trousers, and new socks that Whiley had left him. His rib cage was wrapped tightly, but he managed to get himself dressed. Getting his tall moccasin boots on might be another story. As he walked near the door to them, he heard familiar voices.

John Van Horn's voice came from the next room. "I noticed your new sign out there says *Whiley 'and Sons' Outfitters*," he said. "I didn't know you had sons, Trask."

"I don't. But a man can dream." The men laughed.

Yiska never thought he'd see the day that Trask Whiley would settle down. He'd been more than an employer to him—more like an older brother—but Yiska couldn't picture him as a family man. More than likely Mr. Whiley figured marriage could be a good business venture, and sons would help him carry on his name.

Out in the hallway, Whiley cleared his throat. "John, I'd like to have a word with you about your daughter."

four

What was on Whiley's mind now? He wasn't sweet on Eliana, was he? Yiska felt like someone had kicked him in the gut all over again.

"What's this about Eliana?" Mr. Van Horn examined Mr. Whiley with a suspecting eye while Yiska peered at them from the partially open door of the small room.

"Where *is* your lovely daughter today?" Whiley asked.

"She's shopping in town with a friend. Then off to Richmond's Mercantile to check on the catalog orders that we placed—photography supplies and such—and to pick up some sundries for our expedition with the Robbins survey. We'll get the rest of our supplies from you." Mr. Van Horn glanced around Whiley's store. Shelves and tables were stocked with tack, tents, blankets, lanterns, guns and ammunition, mining tools, building supplies, and even some Indian trade goods. "Have you ever thought of opening a remote outfit up in Lake City?"

"I've considered it." Whiley nodded.

"Would be nice to get supplies closer to home. We won't be back in Del Norte before we leave, so we're gathering our provisions now." Mr. Van Horn rocked back on his heels and smiled. "Our grand adventure is nigh upon us."

"That's exactly what I'm concerned about, John." Mr. Whiley's face grew serious. "I've heard recent reports of renegade bands of Utes south of here, and I wanted to warn you." Whiley leaned with his elbow resting on the counter. "It's none of my business what you do, but I thought you might want to reconsider taking your daughter along on your excursion. You don't want her to end up like that Oatman woman."

Yiska swallowed hard.

"Trask, I appreciate your concern. But we've already given it a lot of thought and prayer. I know you're not a religious man, but we have peace about it. This expedition is the chance of a lifetime for me *and* my daughter." Mr. Van Horn turned and, as if speaking straight to Yiska, said, "You know, Eliana will dress like a young man, the way she does when we go into the mining camps to take pictures. That way no one will be the wiser."

Yiska's jaw dropped. How could John Van Horn even consider allowing Eliana to go? It took more than a little peace and preparation to be equipped for such a journey. Yiska should know—he'd roamed the southwest for most of his life. He shook his head. She'd be dressed like a. . .

"So be it. I know there won't be any changing your minds." Whiley let out a deep chuckle. "Does the U.S. General Land Office know she's coming along?"

"They know I'm bringing an assistant."

"And here I thought you were an honest man," Whiley teased.

Van Horn stroked his beard. "You know I hired a man to go with me on the survey. I couldn't help the fact that he got the gold fever this spring and left me high and dry. The contract never specified that I report any changes. It was too late to back out, and I have an able assistant. But if they get wind. . . I can count on you to keep this detail in confidence, can't I? You're the only other living soul who knows about it." Van Horn took his empty pipe from his pocket and tapped it in the palm of his hand nervously.

"I won't say a word. But you'd better hope that the Utes don't find her out. John, I'm serious."

"You don't have to warn me about the danger of Indians." Mr. Van Horn's mouth drew into a grim line before he worked his pipe between his lips.

"Well, not only that, I've heard that Chandler Robbins isn't one to put up with any nonsense. Make sure Eliana carries her weight, or he may detect she isn't who she claims to be." Whiley shook his head and shrugged. "I hope Eliana *can* shoot a shotgun as well as a camera."

Withdrawing his unlit pipe, Van Horn chortled. "Don't worry. They don't call her 'Eagle Eye Eli' for nothing."

Whiley looked up and caught sight of Yiska standing in the doorway. Yiska issued an obligatory nod and left, his head ready to explode with all that he'd learned. He bolted for the mercantile. How could a man set both his mind and spirit toward a decision and come up with an answer like that? Bringing a young woman into the wilds on a long expedition was dangerous for many reasons. Mr. Van Horn must not be thinking clearly. What kind of God did he believe in? He didn't understand what it was like out there. But Yiska did. And only one thing could be done about it.

He had to stop her.

&

After an hour of shopping and fittings for her friend's new gown, Eliana and Alice headed toward the mercantile at last. As they descended the steps at the end of the boardwalk, Alice's dress caught on a piece of jagged wood.

"Oh, I hope it didn't tear!"

Eliana stooped to release the fabric. "No harm done." The corner of a brown, leather-covered book tied with a rawhide cord stuck out from under the steps. "Look here; someone must have dropped this."

"Open it," Alice said. "How else can we discover to whom it belongs?"

The book was filled will all kinds of descriptive writing. "I think it may be someone's journal." Eliana passed it to Alice.

"There's no name. What shall we do with it?" Alice fingered through some of the pages. "We could keep it. It might make good reading."

"We cannot do that," Eliana chided. "What if the owner is looking for it?"

"What shall we do then?"

"I'll take it to the newspaper tomorrow when I go to place an advertisement. I'll ask the editor to place a special ad to find the owner."

"That seems best." Alice handed Eliana the journal.

Eliana placed the mysterious book in her satchel, and they walked on.

"Good afternoon, ladies," said Mr. Richmond as they entered the mercantile.

"Hello, Mr. Richmond. I came to see if any packages have arrived addressed to Van Horn Photography." Eliana's heart flooded with hope.

"I'll go see what we have for you. A delivery arrived a little while ago. Haven't had a chance to sort it yet."

Alice walked over to the sewing notions. "Oh look, Eliana! This lace ribbon matches the lace on your blue dress perfectly. I didn't notice any like this at Mrs. Donnelly's Dress Shoppe. You should get a length of it for your hair."

"Oh, I don't know. I'm on a budget, and I've spent far too much already." Eliana peeked into her reticule to count her money. "I'd better not, at least until I see how much my other purchases will be."

"But, you must."

Eliana laughed, "Alice, you're rather good at spending my money. But despite your good taste, I must wait."

"Very well." Alice walked toward some bolts of fabric as Eliana made her way toward the soaps and toiletries.

A moment later, Alice sidled up her and whispered, "Did you see that. . .fellow. . .back there? He's looking at you. Look at him!"

"Alice! I will *not* look." Eliana spoke in hushed tones.

"Oh, you must. He's so handsome. . .for an Injun."

Eliana clutched Alice's arm. "What does he look like?"

Alice looked casually over her shoulder, pretending to look about the store. "Well, he's, you know. His skin is very tanned. Dark hair, almost down to his shoulders. He's wearing a slouch hat. He has a buckskin vest and a pair of those high suede boots. And he's grinning."

At that, Eliana turned around. She hadn't realized that Mr. Wilcox was actually in the store. Had he heard their whispers, and Alice's giggles?

Mr. Wilcox nodded. Eliana managed a shy smile. Warmth flamed through her cheeks. She turned back to Alice.

"What is it?" Alice whispered.

"Nothing." Eliana worried her lip.

"Nothing? You know him. You do! I can tell. . . . And you like him."

Oh dear, had he heard Alice say that? Eliana looked at Mr. Wilcox again. He was perusing some books in the corner. *So*, he could read.

In hushed tones Alice continued, "Is he the one?"

Eliana croaked, "Yes. How many Indians do you think I know?"

Alice's mother bustled into the store. "There you are, dear, I've been looking all over for you. You were to meet me back at Mrs. Donnelly's shop after your errands. Come now, I need your help with your sister's dress. She's waiting for us there now."

"But Mother." Alice grimaced and heaved a little sigh.

"Come along now. Good afternoon, Eliana. Our family will be by later in the week for our portrait sitting. See you then, dear."

"Yes, see you then." Alice peeked again at Mr. Wilcox and smirked at Eliana as her mother escorted her out the door.

"Is this what you were waiting for, Miss Van Horn?" Mr. Richmond returned, carrying a carton.

Eliana walked over and placed the sundries she had gathered on the counter. "Is that the only one?"

Mr. Richmond checked his ledger. "The rest of your order hasn't arrived yet. Hmm. Coming all the way from New York. These things take time, sometimes even get lost en route."

"Oh, dear! What if our photography supplies don't arrive

in time? We must have them before we leave Del Norte."

Oh, Lord, please make the equipment get here in time. To her dismay, Mr. Wilcox stood there beside her, concern on his face.

"Thank you, Mr. Richmond. I guess that's all we can do for now. I'll pay for this now, along with these items." She glanced toward the lace ribbon, but she had no need of frippery where she was headed. She took the money from her reticule and placed it on the counter.

The proprietor put his hand on the box and held it there. "Before you go I'd like to check the order, to make sure it's correct. It's the least I can do."

Her eyes darted to Mr. Wilcox. "I'm sure it's all here, Mr. Richmond." Maybe she should tell him the contents were personal. But saying so wouldn't be appropriate in male company. Her heart pounded.

"Miss Van Horn, I insist." He opened the pasteboard container and pulled out three men's shirts and a pair of men's trousers. "Let me check it against the invoice." Mr. Wilcox turned his back and leaned against the counter, arms folded across his chest.

"Three cotton shirts, men's size small, sixty cents each. Two dungarees, boys' size large, a dollar twenty-five. Two pair gents' imitation buckskin gloves, one large, one small, one dollar and fifty cents each."

Eliana's cheeks grew warmer as Mr. Richmond continued his relentless inventory. She stared at the clothing and dared not glance at Mr. Wilcox.

"Men's socks, half dozen each, large and small, forty cents each. Suede vest, men's medium, eight dollars and seventy-five cents. Women's hose, size medium, three pair, a dollar thirty each."

Mr. Wilcox muffled a laugh. Eliana ignored him, her entire face on fire.

"Looks like it's all here as ordered," Richmond said. "Montgomery Ward guarantees complete satisfaction or your money back, and I stand behind that policy. But if I do say so, Miss Van Horn, most of these garments are not going to fit Mr. Van Horn. Much too small."

"They are not for him, Mr. Richmond. They are for. . . somebody else."

"A gift? That's mighty generous."

Eliana resisted the urge to bolt for the door. "Well, yes, they are much needed by the person who'll receive them. Please, if you would package them back up again, I'll be on my way. And please be sure to let us know the moment our other boxes arrive."

"Yes, miss, I know you need them before your trip."

Eliana felt as if all her secrets had been exposed, though she knew it wasn't true.

"Trip. Yes. Before we return to Lake City."

Mr. Wilcox turned and faced her. "May I be of assistance, Miss Van Horn? I can carry your packages for you."

The proprietor looked at Eliana and noted her discomfort. He stood a little straighter. "Don't you be bothering her now. If you have some business of your own here, you can stay. Otherwise be on your way."

"Mr. Richmond, this gentleman is no bother at all. In fact, I will take him up on his helpful offer."

"Very well, if you're certain."

"I've never been more certain of anything in my life. Good day."

Mr. Wilcox carried her package as they walked out of the store. My, he looked like he was in pain.

"Do you get treated like that everywhere you go, Mr. Wilcox?"

"Enough."

"But you are only half Indian from what I understand."

"It's the wrong half."

"Well, it isn't right. Just because you look like. . .I mean. . . You don't really look that much like an Indian. It's just your coloring, and your hair. And that tomahawk—your hatchet. . ."

Was she so nervous in his presence that she couldn't utter a decent sentence?

"Would it be a *bad* thing if I did look like a full-blooded Indian, Miss Van Horn?"

"Of course it would. It would be bad for you." Her eyes widened. "Especially since you're innocent." Eliana bit her lip. She didn't mean that like it sounded.

"Innocent?" Mr. Wilcox set her packages down on a bench out front and leaned against a post.

She sat down and looked up at him apologetically. "I don't mean to imply that Indians are inherently bad. *All* human beings are sinful from birth. And everyone has their faults." *Haven't I proved my own by muddling up this conversation?* "But for others to assume that you are a savage is simply ludicrous."

"Is it?"

She couldn't read his expression any more than she could see through a Colorado blizzard, but Eliana could tell by his tone that she'd offended him. "Yes, of course. Since I have met you, you've been nothing but courteous to me. You saved my life, for mercy's sake!"

"And you mine. At least you considered mine worth the saving."

"And I do, Mr. Wilcox. You are a valuable human being, despite the way you are sometimes treated. I hope you never forget that."

"Your good opinion of me is all that matters."

A large, scruffy dog ran by with something in its mouth. "You get outta there!" Mrs. Sanborn's husband hollered at the animal and whacked him with a broom handle.

"Did you see that?" Eliana asked. "The poor dog was just hungry. He didn't do a thing!"

Mr. Wilcox's jaw tightened. "Some people can't tell the difference between a good dog and a bad dog."

Eliana clamped her lips together, eyeing him apologetically. "I'd best be on my way," he said, "unless I can see you somewhere. To Whiley's outfitting company perhaps? Your father was there."

"He asked me to wait for him here."

"All right, Miss Van Horn. It's been a pleasure as always." He tipped his hat.

"I hope you'll come by to have your photograph taken. It would please my father very much if you would."

"Would it please *you*, Miss Van Horn?"

She blushed. Why did he have to be so direct? "Yes, it would, Mr. Wilcox." It would indeed.

❧

Yiska returned to the outfitting company through the front door. As he entered he glanced up at the sign, WHILEY OUTFITTERS AND SONS. He thought of his relief at learning Whiley didn't seem to have it in mind to marry Eliana. Why should it matter to him? It wasn't like Yiska had staked a claim on her.

"Look what the wind rolled in. Yiska, what are you doing up and about? Feeling any better, son?" Mr. Whiley asked.

"Some."

"Saw you up a little while ago. Where'd you go? John and I went to get a bite at Sanborn's. I was going to ask if I could bring back something for you, but you'd disappeared. Brought you a plate anyway."

Mr. Van Horn smacked his lips. "Turkey sandwiches and gingerbread today."

"Sounds great. Thank you." Yiska rubbed his side. "I went for a walk."

"Doc said you need to rest up if you want to fully recover."

Mr. Van Horn raised a brow. "You were hurt worse than you let on."

Whiley scowled. "He had another run-in with that Grover character and his buddy."

"Oh?"

"I was out looking for something that was stolen from me the other day, and I ran into him. Hard. He tried to finish the job he'd started at the sawmill."

"Yiska ended up with a couple of cracked ribs. But he had the last word, so to speak."

Yiska eyed the map spread out on the table. "What've you got here?"

"This is the route for the Robbins survey of the four corners and down the New Mexico and Arizona border. Mr. Van Horn has been assigned as the official photographer for the expedition."

"How'd you come by that deal, Mr. Van Horn? If you don't mind me asking."

"Not at all. I served with Chandler Robbins during the war—Ohio's 86th Infantry. Served alongside James Ryder as well. He's now a famed photographer back East. I was his assistant during the war and for some time at home. That's how I got my start—brutal as it was. When Robbins approached him about the survey project, he couldn't do it but recommended me instead. Perfect opportunity since I already do contract work for the General Land Office regionally."

As the men leaned over the map, Yiska looked on.

Mr. Whiley traced the route and laid out the itinerary. "Once you make your way down the Animas River and through the Ute reservation, you'll cross the border into New Mexico—Navajo territory. You should be relatively safe there." Whiley glanced at Yiska then continued the itinerary. "You'll continue along the Animas until you come to a confluence of three rivers. There you'll continue on the Rio San Juan. You'll be heading west toward Shiprock." He jabbed the map with his finger. "The coordinates are marked here at the four corners quadripoint."

Mr. Van Horn rested his hands on his hips. "What about the ruins? How will I find them?"

"I have them marked here, and here." Whiley pointed to the various locations. "Besides, your guide will know the area well." Mr. Van Horn looked at Yiska and flattened his lips.

Why did he look so disappointed?

"Mr. Van Horn, I almost forgot to mention that I saw your daughter at the mercantile when I was out."

Van Horn peered up at Yiska over his spectacles. "Do you happen to know if our packages arrived?"

"From what I gathered, eh, only the clothing order."

Mr. Van Horn frowned. "I see. Well, I promised I'd pick her up with a wagon. I had better get over there now." He straightened as Whiley rolled up a copy of the map and handed it to him. "Make sure you stop by the studio, young man. I'd like to see you again before we go."

"Yes, sir." Why did he feel like he'd be saying his final farewell?

When Mr. Van Horn left, Whiley rolled up the other copies of the map. Yiska turned his thoughts back to the expedition. "It'll be good to get back down to New Mexico Territory again. It's been too long. Does Mr. Van Horn know that I'll be along as the guide?"

Whiley exhaled. "Well, Yiska, plans have changed. . . . You won't be going on that expedition."

five

Eliana paused outside the *San Juan Prospector* to enjoy the grand views—the flat plain, grassy meadows, and stunning vista. To the east lay a sandy desert, and to the west the grand San Juan Mountains, full of promise and adventure. She pulled in a deep breath, entered the large sandstone building, and addressed the clerk. "I'd like to see Mr. Wilson, please."

A neatly dressed man entered the front room, wiping ink-stained hands with a clean rag. "Miss Van Horn, it's a pleasure to see you." He examined his fingers. "Having a little trouble with the printing press."

"Are you still accepting advertisements today?"

"Certainly. It's business as usual. Nothing stops the *San Juan Prospector* from going to press."

"I have a few things I'd like to discuss with you," she said with a smile.

"Snivens, show Miss Van Horn to my office while I finish cleaning my hands. Make sure she's comfortable."

Mr. Snivens ushered Eliana into a large office and seated her in a tufted leather chair across from a large mahogany desk. Such exquisite furniture. What would it be like to have such luxury? Eliana only wished Papa's hard work would reap similar benefits. She would like to see him enjoy some measure of comfort in his lifetime.

"Now, what can I help you with today?" The older man settled into his oversized chair.

Eliana placed a paper on the desk. "First of all, I would like to place another advertisement for Van Horn Photography in your paper. Father and I will only be here a little while longer, and we want to make sure that everyone in the community who would like to have their photograph taken will have the opportunity. We are hosting a special on family portraits."

"I'll see to it." Wilson settled back in his chair. "I'm glad you dropped by today. I understand that your father will be heading out to visit The Silver Queen before he embarks on his expedition."

"I take it you mean Silverton?" Eliana asked.

"Indeed, I do. I'd like to get a picture of a Mr. Francis Snowden at the mine. He was the first to put up a cabin and stake a claim in that flourishing town, and he's the only surviving member of the Baker party, who discovered the mineral deposits there. I have a correspondent headed that way to conduct an interview. But a photograph would be a nice addition to the story."

"I'm sure he'd be honored to do that for you, Mr. Wilson."

"Very well, then. I look forward to printing the engravings of the Robbins survey when he returns. You must be very proud of your father."

Eliana beamed. "Oh, yes, sir. I am. But you know that the U.S. General Land Office has first rights to the photographs."

"A mere technicality. I'll handle the GLO." Wilson glanced at the pendulum clock on the wall. "You had something else?"

"Mr. Wilson, I happen to be in possession of an important document. Perhaps you could help me locate the owner. You may already know to whom this belongs." Eliana placed the leather-bound journal on the mahogany desk.

Mr. Wilson arched his brow. "May I?"

"Please do. This journal is filled with pages of very eloquent prose describing the vast wilderness of the territory. And there is no name to be found. I'd like to place an advertisement seeking its proper owner."

Mr. Wilson put on his eyeglasses and examined the book. He fumbled through some of the pages, landing midway. His eyes scanned the page. He cleared his throat and read aloud.

The ravine sings to the tune of a thousand stars above. The night in no way diminishes the glory of this place, but rather illuminates a view that remains hidden in the day. The moon above shines down on white-capped mountains, a beacon urging me to come near. As I travel forward on frozen ground, large flakes cling to my garments and will soon cover the ground like a woolen blanket. My shelter lies near, a cave, and fresh pine boughs for my bed. A flickering spark is all that I will need to ignite a small fire and regenerate the warmth I once felt in late spring. Should an avalanche usher me to an early end, I am grateful for having sojourned under such a majestic and heavenly night.

Eliana sighed. "I regret having intruded on this individual's private world, but. . ."

"Miss Van Horn, you have done a great deed by bringing this to me." The editor held up the journal to the light of the window, the San Juan Mountains visible in the distance. "This world needs to be shared!"

જ

The chill in the air penetrated Yiska's aching ribs through his buckskin coat. He'd hoped to be feeling better by now—or was it Mr. Whiley's announcement that still wounded him? Chilled him. How could his boss refuse to let him go on the survey expedition? Whiley knew that Yiska was more familiar with that territory than anyone else. It was on the Navajo reservation, after all.

Only the other day he'd wondered how he could prevent the adventurous Miss Van Horn from going on the trip. But at least if he was there he could help keep her safe. . .and keep her secret. He'd also get to spend time with her. Of course, she'd be safer still if she didn't go at all.

He hadn't managed to find an opportunity to talk to her about halting her plans for the trip. When he saw how disappointed she'd been about the missing photography supplies, he hadn't had the heart to discourage her further.

Instead, when he'd gone back to purchase some new clothing and a journal, he bought her that slip of ribbon. What was he thinking? If he couldn't find a way to talk her out of the trip, how would he ever manage to offer her a small gift? He sighed. No use dwelling on it. Mr. Richmond's peculiar look at Yiska was punishment enough for his impulsive act.

But perhaps giving her the lace would make her more receptive to considering his concern for her. Obviously she hadn't fully thought about the dangers. Maybe he would be able to speak with her today.

He stepped into Van Horn's photography studio in a store front next to the bakery. From the corner of the room he watched Eliana as she posed her friend's family for a portrait. Alice's mother was seated, and her father stood behind her, hand on her shoulder. Alice and a younger sister stood on their mother's left, while two boys stood on the opposite side by their father. A backdrop of a painted mountain landscape completed the scene.

"Andrew and Angus, you must keep still. If you keep smiling, your faces will be blurred in the picture. Now please cooperate and keep your mouths closed. If you do, I've a gumdrop for each of you."

Yiska had seen those boys before. Weren't they the ones who had called him names in front of Eliana last week? He slipped out and decided to go to the bakery to pass the time until they were finished.

Once he knew they had gone, he returned to the studio with two raspberry turnovers wrapped in a cloth napkin. Miss Van Horn bent over a table with a paintbrush in hand. "Mr. Wilcox, I'm glad you came by."

"I was at the bakery and thought to bring you a snack." He set the pastries on the table.

"How thoughtful. And these are my favorite!" Miss Van Horn walked over to an elegant tea service in the corner of the room. "Do you drink tea, Mr. Wilcox?"

"Yes." He looked at the table where Eliana had been

working. "What are you doing over there?"

"I'm hand tinting some ferrotypes. Color adds a little life to their faces, don't you agree? I've some photographs to develop as well. It's been such a busy week. Townsfolk are making sure they come see us before we are on our way again. We won't be back in Del Norte for some time."

Yiska looked around the room. "No, I reckon you won't." A display table caught his attention. He pointed to a celluloid panel with four identical miniature portraits. "What do you call these?"

"Four ferrotypes to a panel are called *bon tons*."

"That's a peculiar name. What do people do with such small pictures?"

"They put them in lockets or in miniature albums like these." Eliana picked up a small, ornate book and opened it to show pages of tiny pictures inside. "The actual photographs are referred to as gems. These show many of our clients over the years who have been gracious enough to let us have a sample."

"Gems. This one is of you." *A beautiful jewel.* On the table beside them, Yiska noticed another picture of Miss Van Horn. He picked it up. As he held it he imagined what it would be like to hold her in his arms. *But why dream something that will never be?*

"That's a cabinet card. Papa took that one of me a few weeks back in the new dress he bought for me."

"I remember that dress. You had it on the first day we met." Why'd he have to say that? Now she was blushing.

"Since you're here, you must allow me to take your portrait—a cabinet card. Don't be shy. People have their pictures taken all the time. Have you ever had yours made?"

"No, can't say that I have."

Miss Van Horn glanced over his outfit and smiled. "Are you wearing new clothes?"

He nodded. Did she think he had dressed up to come see her?

"Perfect. See, you are all dressed for a sitting. You must agree," she said.

How can I say no to such a charmer? "All right. On one condition."

Miss Van Horn tilted her pretty head. "And what, Mr. Wilcox, is that?"

"Do I look like a Mr. Wilcox to you? Please call me Yiska."

"Then come this way, Yiska." She turned her head back over her shoulder. "Oh, and you must call me Eliana."

❧

Eliana had almost spilled the pigments when she looked up and saw Mr. Wilcox—Yiska—enter the studio. How ruggedly handsome he looked in his fringed leather coat. He took his hat off and hung it on a hook by the door, his dark hair framing his chiseled features. And now she would finally get to take his photograph.

Eliana began to move one of the chairs away from the sitting area when Yiska placed his hand on hers.

"Allow me." He gazed directly into her eyes. "All of them?"

"All but one. They can go over there against the wall." As he put the chairs away, she said, "I'm so glad you stopped by today. Papa will be pleased."

"I wanted to see the shadow catcher's daughter again before you left Del Norte."

Eliana's curiosity piqued. "Shadow catcher?"

"That's what Indians call photographers. Will I see your father today?"

"He's in town, but I expect him back anytime."

"Good. He asked that I stop by, but I do have something that I'd like to talk to you both about."

"All right. But now let's get you situated for the photograph. Please place that chair directly in the center of the backdrop."

Yiska positioned the chair per her direction.

"Now, you may sit down."

Yiska turned the chair around, its back facing the camera, and straddled it.

Eliana giggled. "All right then, have it your way. For now."

"That's my aim," he said with a grin.

Eliana tilted her head one way and then the other. "Would you mind, Mr. Wil—Yiska—if I fixed your hair? You have a slight issue of indentations from your hat."

"Whatever you please."

Eliana grabbed a comb from her pocket and proceeded to flatten the subtle bumps. She hadn't realized his hair would be so thick.

He looked up at her. "You could always let me wear my hat."

"No, I think it will be better without it." Eliana recalled the first time she saw him—his hat was missing. In this close proximity, the scent of rich, new leather tickled her senses. How good he smelled. "Yiska, I think you ought to remove your coat."

"That won't be as easy as you think," he confessed. "I'm healing up from a couple of bruised ribs."

"Why didn't you tell me? I let you move those chairs."

"It's not the kind of thing a man likes to brag about."

Eliana could tell by the way he glanced away that she shouldn't press for an explanation. She hoped his injury wasn't from those big-booted ruffians who had taken him to jail.

"No harm done. Now, if you could help me off with my coat, that'd be mighty nice of you."

Eliana stood behind him and carefully pulled the coat as he released his arms from one sleeve and then the other. She laid it down on a chair, her heart aflutter. Gracious. She'd never been so intimate with a man in her life. She looked toward the front door, wishing she could go out and get a breath of fresh air. She walked over to retrieve Yiska's hat from its hook and peeked out the window. What was taking Papa so long?

"What next?"

"Well. . .we must position you for the photograph. I'd rather you sat in the other direction please and place your hat on your knee. Sometimes we like to give our subjects props, and I cannot think of a more suitable one for you."

Yiska adjusted himself accordingly.

Eliana gingerly placed her hands on his sturdy shoulders to square them, his warmth passing through her fingers. Thoughts rushed into her head of the last time she had been this close to him—the day he had helped her down from Mr. Whiley's buckboard, and she thought he might kiss her.

She pushed a loose tendril of hair from her face and regained her bearings. "Now, when I go over to the camera to take the picture, you must remain perfectly still or the picture will be blurred, and we'll have to go through all of this again." She couldn't endure it.

"How do I look?"

"You look very handsome." *Did I really say that?* She was accustomed to complimenting her subjects, but not under these circumstances. Oh, how could she?

Yiska smiled.

Oh, but he had a nice mouth. And his eyes. "Mr. Wilcox, you mustn't smile, or it will ruin everything." She noticed a speck of jam from the raspberry turnover on his face.

"You. . .you have a bit of raspberry on your face." Eliana pointed to his chin. "You know, they used raspberry syrup in the old days to keep the camera's glass plates wet. We mostly use dry plates now."

"Tintypes."

"Yes, although they are actually made from iron."

"I see." Yiska wiped his face, and then again, missing the spot both times.

"No, here." Eliana dabbed it away, blushing.

She turned and hastened to her camera, pulling the black tarp over her head before he could see that her face had probably reddened to the color of that raspberry jam. She wanted to remain there forever, but no. . . . She regained her composure and looked through the viewfinder. "Mr. Wilcox! Please do not smile."

Yiska seemed eager to watch her develop the photographs.

His interest in the procedure seemed genuine. Eliana was glad to answer his questions, but she simply couldn't allow him to be alone with her in the darkroom. He waited in the sitting area, and her thoughts swirled so much she could barely breathe by the time the processing was completed.

A short time later Eliana emerged from the darkroom and handed Yiska the finished product.

"Thank you. But I don't know what I'll do with it." Yiska walked over to the display table and picked up the small portrait of her. "How about a trade?"

Eliana's pulse quickened. "That sounds fair." They stood silently for a moment, admiring one another's images.

"Good news!" Papa waddled into the studio carrying a huge box. "Our supplies have arrived! We can leave any day now."

And when they did, apart from his photograph, would Eliana ever lay eyes on Yiska again?

six

Trask Whiley watched Yiska count out the boxes of ammunition. Yiska looked up. "Fifteen Henry rifles, eighteen Winchesters, and fifty rounds for each. You could stand to get a dozen more traps. I've written it all down."

"You've got a good head for business, Yiska. Perhaps I should keep you off the trail and have you work here in the store instead."

Although Yiska missed being out in the territory, he didn't mind staying at the store for a bit to take stock of the outfitting company's inventory. "You'll need to increase your supplies of mining equipment, too. They're coming in droves."

"How're your ribs healing up?"

"Much better now, though I can't lift anything heavy yet."

"Glad you can still lift a pencil. You've been mighty handy around here lately." Whiley placed a hand on Yiska's shoulder. "Time to take a break."

They sat on the front porch, sipping cups of strong coffee. Whiley targeted a nearby spittoon. How Mr. Whiley drank and chewed at the same time, Yiska would never know. He kicked back, stretched out his legs, and pulled his hat over his eyes while Whiley browsed *The Prospector* for the competition's advertising.

"Richmond is selling mining supplies now, too. He's got pickaxes and shovels for two bits apiece under my price. What does he mean by underselling me? I'm going over there."

He left *The Prospector* sitting on the wooden bench, and Yiska caught it as it was about to blow away. He looked at the front page, catching a headline—HAYDEN CONTINUES TO SURVEY WESTERN LOOP. Soon enough Chandler Robbins would be making the headlines. Yiska hoped they wouldn't read FEMALE PHOTOGRAPHER CAPTURED BY UTES. If Eliana was going on that expedition, he had to find a way to go as well.

As he flipped through the pages he couldn't get Eliana's pretty face, her bright hazel eyes, and hair the color of a fawn out of his mind. Nor could he remove the image of her lovely feminine form, the way she moved, the scent of lavender that wafted through the air in her presence—or the yearning that he had to explore the territory of her heart.

Another headline snagged his attention. Yiska could hardly believe his eyes. An article had been published under the pseudonym, "Anonymous Explorer." He skimmed it, his pulse rocketing as he read. It was an entry from his missing journal! A glance at the print ending the column told him this was not the first but the second entry from a journal that had been turned in to the newspaper's editor, Mr. Wilson, and that Wilson was eager to make the acquaintance of its owner.

Yiska jumped to his feet, paced the porch, then whacked his hat against the post. This was his prized journal, his faithful companion, and his hope to become accredited as a travel correspondent in the Southwest. He'd planned to submit some of his entries to a newspaper in the East—one which did not have the "benefit" of knowing his heritage. Mr. Wilson would never believe it if Yiska came forward to reveal that the journal belonged to him. He looked at his hat, now all dented. He needed someone who could speak on his behalf. He'd better track down Trask Whiley.

"Now you're talking sense, Richmond." As he went into the mercantile, Yiska found Mr. Whiley "negotiating" with Mr. Richmond. He turned to Yiska. "What is it?" he barked.

"I need your help," Yiska said.

Whiley exhaled and held up his hand. "All right." He looked back at Richmond. "I believe we've come to an understanding." Whiley stomped into the street and started walking. "So what is it? Don't mean to be impatient. He just got my dander up."

&

"Good afternoon, Miss Alice." Mr. Van Horn said.

"How do you do, Mr. Van Horn? Is Eliana here?"

"I'm right here, Alice." Eliana lifted her head from behind the counter. "I'm packing our supplies." She wiped the perspiration from her forehead. "Your photographs are done. I'm glad you stopped by."

Mr. Van Horn smiled at Alice as he stepped aside to let her enter. "And they came out quite well, I might add. It's getting harder all the time to tell the difference between my talented daughter's photographs and my own."

"She's one special girl," Alice said. "I'm sure going to miss her. Eliana, do you have time for tea at Mrs. Sanborn's café?"

"Well, I don't know. . . ."

"Sure she does," her father said. "I've been working her hard enough."

At the café Mrs. Sanborn served Eliana and Alice a pot of hot tea with some warm apple muffins and a fresh bit of gossip. "That anonymous author in *The Prospector* is the talk of the town. He has all the men hankering to get out into the mountains and all the women practically swooning." The girls giggled as Mrs. Sanborn walked away to serve another table with the same dish.

"I wish you could stay longer." A forlorn sigh escaped Alice's pouty lips.

"We can correspond. Lake City opened a post office. Please don't act like you'll never see me again."

"Perhaps I won't. You'll probably become a famous female photographer and run off with that Indian."

"Alice! Mind your imagination. I'll do no such thing."

Alice's eyes grew mischievous. "You can't tell me that you haven't at least thought of it."

Eliana looked down. Her cheeks must be all shades of red. She looked up at Alice and burst into giggles, quickly covering her mouth.

"I knew it! Your secret is safe with me. And your other one also."

Eliana feigned innocence. "What do you mean?" Could she possibly know?

Alice declared in a soft voice, "Eliana Van Horn, you have been disguising yourself as a man!"

Eliana grabbed Alice's hand. "Shhhh! I cannot believe you know! Please, Alice, you cannot tell a living soul. Papa only agrees to it for my protection." She dared not mention the expedition.

"I won't breathe a word. I would never want any harm to come to you." Alice blotted her napkin against her lips. "Now, how about confessing your undying love for that Yiska fellow."

"Alice, I do not love Yiska. Not in that way. I only care for him as I would any of God's children."

"Is he a child of God, Eliana, or is he a heathen?" Alice asked.

Eliana wished she knew. There was a long silence.

Alice mouthed the words. "Has he ever kissed you?"

"Kissed me? I hardly know him." But she had thought about it. Did that count?

Eliana was relieved when Alice picked up the newspaper that had been left behind on a vacant table. "Oh, look! There's another article by the Anonymous Explorer. Listen to this:

> The sand shifts like shadows underneath my tired feet.
> Though paths are worn before me, some I have trod alone
> and beckon others to follow. The cliffs rise to tell legends from
> days of old. And tales anew I write, to share these wonders
> with those who might otherwise have never known.

Eliana and Alice sighed in perfect harmony. Alice placed her hand against her chest. "Isn't the author romantic?"

"Beyond compare. Now that is one I could spend my

dreams on. Yet I can't help but feel that I had a hand in betraying his confidence, by giving over his journal only to see it end up in print. Those reflections are immensely personal." Eliana also felt a pang of guilt that these thoughts had betrayed her feelings for Yiska.

"You needn't feel bad. How do you know that you haven't done the author a good deed?"

❧

"Look here, Wilson. I've known this young man for more than ten years. He's like a son to me. I know, I know—you're thinking a half breed can't possibly write like that. But my own mother schooled him herself when he lived with them. I know firsthand that he can read and write better than I can." Mr. Whiley walked toward the window to cool down and faced Wilson again. "Read just one sentence of any one of those entries, and he can tell you what happened next. He knows all those places like the back of his hand. As a matter of fact, he should be compensated for those articles."

"Here now, Whiley. I've never known you to be a dishonest man. I'll take your word for it." Mr. Wilson looked at Yiska, confounded. "Young man, have a seat."

Mr. Wilson rocked back in his chair. "Yiska, you've captured your audience with the enthusiasm of dime novels. I'd like to print the rest of your journal. In fact, I've already taken the liberty of having it copied. And I'd like to see more. Of course, for now you'll continue to be hailed as the 'Anonymous Explorer.' We've got newspapers to sell."

How this disaster turned into a writing job, Yiska didn't know. And had Mr. Whiley really said that Yiska was like a son to him? After ironing out some of the particulars for his compensation and future publication, Mr. Wilson offered another proposition. "One of my correspondents suddenly came down with the measles. I need someone capable to handle an assignment for me out in the San Juans. Silverton. It's an interview with Francis Snowden." He slid a piece of paper across the desk toward Yiska. "The details are right here. What do you say, Mr. Wilcox?"

"I'd be happy to do it, sir."

Yiska stood and shook Mr. Wilson's hand then turned to shake Whiley's, who offered his support. Yiska would still be a trail guide, but he would now have the added pleasure of writing about what he saw for pay. Things couldn't have turned out better.

Wilson took Yiska's journal out of a desk drawer. "I believe this belongs to you."

Yiska held it with both hands. "Thank you, Mr. Wilson. I feel like I've been reunited with an old friend."

"One more thing. I've hired someone to take a picture of Snowden to accompany the interview. You might even meet up with them out there. Van Horn Photography. Do you know them?"

seven

Eliana pulled the shawl around her shoulders and yawned as she waited with her father at the station agent's window at Barlow & Sanderson's Overland Stage & Express Line. The mixture of the chilled morning air and her eagerness to be under way perked her awake. She looked forward to going home to Lake City and seeing her friends, though their time there would be brief and busy with further preparation—the expedition now only weeks away. Only one thing lingered on her mind, and soon she could leave that thought behind her.

"Two tickets. Del Norte to Lake City," Papa said.

The station agent motioned to the attendant to weigh the trunk and cartons filled with their photography equipment.

The attendant grabbed the trunk stamped Van Horn Photography. "What's in here, mining tools?" Obviously the man couldn't read.

"Easy with that—it's fragile," said Eliana's father.

"Ain't stamped fragile."

Papa tapped the trunk. "Right there. Fragile. Now go easy."

The attendant nodded and moved with great care. Did he think it was full of explosives? No matter. If he dropped that trunk with her father's expensive equipment inside, there'd be an explosion one way or another. Though usually a patient man, Papa's ire would certainly rise if the tools of his livelihood were damaged. He'd spent a good deal on his new equipment, and it was going to cost him a great deal to get it home.

"Two passengers. Eighty miles each. That'll be a grand total of forty dollars and fifty cents," the agent said.

Eliana gasped. But Papa would recoup his investment once he got paid for his work as a technician on the Robbins survey.

The man looked at Eliana over his spectacles then addressed her father. "That's twelve dollars each and twenty-two cents a pound for your extra baggage. You'll pay for your meals along the way. Full meals are two bits each."

Papa retrieved the payment from his wallet and placed several paper notes and a couple of pieces of silver on the counter.

The station agent stamped their tickets and turned to the attendant. "What are you waiting for? Take that baggage out to the Concord. It pulls out of here at five o'clock sharp."

Eliana adjusted her bonnet and took note of the other passengers waiting to board the stagecoach. How many passengers would travel with them? A middle-aged couple and another rather stocky man with several carpetbags stood nearby. The grease in the gentleman's hair would be covered in dust by the time they arrived at the relay station. At least Papa remembered not to apply his own Thompson's Magnificent Hair Tonic for Men today. He looked better without it.

Eliana listened as the woman read the rules of The Barlow & Sanderson's Stage & Express Line from her brochure to her traveling companions. "Are you armed, dear? These rules are quite specific. . . . 'Firearms may be kept on your person for use in emergencies. Do not fire them for pleasure or shoot at wild animals, as the sound riles the horses. In the event of runaway horses remain calm. Leaping from the coach in panic will leave you injured, at the mercy of the elements, highwaymen, hostile Indians, and hungry coyotes.'" The woman's jaw dangled open.

"A necessary precaution, dear. I have my gun right inside my coat."

Papa cupped his pocket watch in the palm of his hand and noted the time. "Let's go, Sunshine."

The woman patted her husband's arm and scrunched her face up to his. "Aw, did you hear that, dear? He calls his daughter 'Sunshine.'" The man humored her with a pasted-on grin.

Eliana's heart warmed. Her father had called her Sunshine ever since she was a little girl. In the years following her mother's passing, Papa constantly reminded her that she was like the sunshine ever brightening his days. Even though she was now nearly twenty years old, he still called her the endearing name every now and again.

Papa took her by the elbow, and she stepped up into the small compartment of the vermilion-red stagecoach. He handed her his rifle. As she settled in, she pulled Yiska's picture from her reticule to take a quick peek before her father got on board. She couldn't help but wonder where Yiska was now, and if he ever thought of her. Their lives had collided in a providential way, but she had no way of knowing to what end.

⁂

"Mornin', Lucky Jim." Yiska loaded his saddlebags into the rear boot and climbed up to fasten the rest of his gear on top.

"What gives us the pleasure of your company, my good friend?"

"Shadow's up at Rio Grande Pass. Came down lame. Figured a bumpy ride on your rig would beat dealing with that loaned mount I had." Yiska smiled. "Besides, I'm nursing a couple of cracked ribs."

"How'd you come by those?" the driver asked.

"Guess I'm not as lucky as you." Yiska finished tying down the rest of his gear.

"Glad to have you aboard this fine day. How's about ridin' shotgun? Lazy Eddie was otherwise detained, so I'm solo today. It'll be an easy ride—no mail or payroll on board."

The large trunk strapped to the top of the coach caught Yiska's attention—VAN HORN PHOTOGRAPHY. He heard the familiar voice of John Van Horn boom through the air like a cannon. "Yiska Wilcox!"

"Mr. Van Horn." Yiska smiled. "Didn't expect to see you here, sir."

"Our supplies finally arrived, and we were anxious to get a move on." Van Horn stuck his pipe into his pocket.

Yiska's mind galloped ahead.

"Eliana is inside the coach. I'm sure she'll be pleased to see you. You *are* planning to ride inside?"

Yiska looked up at Lucky Jim.

"Looks like today's your lucky day, Yiska. You wouldn't want to disappoint that pretty young lady." He winked.

"Now don't be putting ideas in that fella's head," Van Horn said. Sounded like he wasn't too keen on the idea of anyone being interested in his daughter—especially Yiska.

"This whippersnapper would be blind as a bat if he hadn't already noticed that perty daughter of yours. Go on then and get in. I haven't got all day." Lucky Jim's laughter filled the air.

Yiska climbed aboard with a big grin and put his rifle underneath his seat. He took off his hat and greeted Eliana. "Miss Van Horn. Good to see you again." Would she be as happy to see him?

"Yiska. This is surely a surprise." Eliana's cheeks blushed pink.

"Yes, a pleasant one. Your father said you're headed back already. Looks like I'll have the pleasure of your company once again." Yiska leaned back in his seat, quite content to gaze across at her.

Eliana tilted her dimpled chin. "I must say that I'm surprised to see you take the stage. Don't you prefer to ride?"

"I was outnumbered. Doc said I wasn't fit for riding horseback quite yet, and Mr. Whiley insisted I take the stage." *Did Whiley know the Van Horns would be on this stage?* "You can't tell me the ride will be any smoother, but at least I'll get back to my own horse up at Rio Grande Pass a bit sooner. Shadow might not even remember me, I've been away so long."

The door to the stagecoach opened once more. A large man glared at Yiska and growled. "It seems overcrowded in there."

"What do you mean? Let me see." A woman with a shrill voice pushed past the man. "Ooh," she gasped, looking at

Yiska with alarm. "They didn't say that wild Indians would be riding *with* us!"

Eliana straightened, her mouth hanging agape.

"Now wait just a minute," Mr. Van Horn said.

The woman ignored them and turned to her husband. "When is the next stage?"

"Not for another week, dear."

"We can't wait that long. Why they don't bring a train out this way I don't know." The woman shook her head frantically. Then in a loud whisper she said in her husband's ear, "I thought you said the Indians were put on the reservations."

Yiska sighed. Some fights were not worth picking, and this was an old one. He tried to keep his voice pleasant. "I'll ride up top, ma'am, if it would make you more comfortable."

"I should hope so." The man folded his arms across his broad chest, frowning.

As Yiska removed himself from the coach, he overheard the woman. "He spoke English, dear. I didn't know they could do that."

Yiska climbed to the driver's box and found a spot beside Lucky Jim.

"So you'll be riding shotgun after all." The burly driver handed Yiska a sawed-off shotgun. "Can't be too careful." Lucky Jim looked straight ahead. "G-long! H'up, there!" He cracked the braided whip, and with a jolt the four-in-hand lunged forward.

Reins threaded through his fingers, the driver guided the horses with gentle but firm control. "We call the reins 'ribbons.' This is how I talk to the horses."

Ribbons. Yiska slid his hand into his pocket and toyed with a piece of lace ribbon between his fingers. Would he ever have the nerve to give it to Eliana? Or to give her his heart? And even if she did return his feelings, how could he ever ask her to live the life of an outcast?

❧

How ironic that Yiska, a perfect gentleman, rode above

instead of these ignoramuses. Eliana hoped the crotchety woman appreciated his thoughtfulness, though she knew that was doubtful.

Sixteen miles west and two and a half hours later, the stagecoach arrived at the South Fork relay station in record time, without incident. While the hostlers changed out the horses for a new team, the travelers took their reprieve with coffee and johnnycakes served by the station agent's wife.

"We're going south to Pagosa Springs now," the woman told her. "We'll try a soak in the hot springs there."

How thankful Eliana was to learn that the trio of tourists would not continue the journey northwest with them. The ride from Del Norte had been nothing short of a nightmare. The woman, squeezed between Eliana and the window, had fidgeted almost the entire way and complained of motion sickness. To Eliana's great relief, nothing ever came of it.

The woman's husband and the other gentleman had filled up the opposite bench and shared a flask of bottled merriment, becoming more obnoxious with each passing mile. They had offered some to her father, and though Papa wasn't a drinking man, she couldn't help but wonder if he was tempted if only to put up with the unpleasant ride.

At last, the passengers had dozed off. The couple both snored while their stocky companion's head practically hung out the window. When the man descended the coach, his dusty hair looked like a powdered wig.

At least that ordeal was over.

As the lady departed to board the new coach that had pulled into the station, she leaned toward Eliana and whispered much too loudly, "Be careful of that Indian." Yiska was looking right at them.

Eliana lowered her gaze.

She braced herself as the stagecoach jerked forward and pulled out of the swing station. Papa sat beside her on the padded leather seat, and Yiska now joined them, facing them from the opposite bench. A knife was strapped to his calf.

His hatchet hung from his hip. No wonder the woman was intimidated by Yiska's presence.

The rumbling of the wheels and clopping hooves of the four horses reverberated around them. Dusty particles floated through the air. Inside the coach, an awkward quiet descended. Eliana rolled up the canvas curtain and buckled it. As the stagecoach traveled the toll road along the Rio Grande, she took in the lush view of the river and the great expanse of the mountains all around them. Lulled by the rocking motion, thoughts of the land and its people filled her mind.

Through the years, many had fought over the Colorado Territory, but since the treaty with the Utes, whites had flooded into the area to claim the mineral-rich mountains and rivers. She recalled how proud she was of Papa when he was commissioned to make a glass-plate of the Ute Chief Ouray, who negotiated for the Utes' peace. Papa was very impressed by the man. He had told her how the government wasn't upholding its end of the Brunot Treaty. No wonder the Utes were still hostile at times.

Sometimes she felt like a trespasser in the land, yet it was home to her now. What was it like to have one's homeland confiscated? Where was Yiska's home? She thought of her own ancestors and sighed. She sat up straight, her hands in her lap, and addressed her traveling companion. "So, Mr. Wilcox."

He looked at her with his dark, penetrating eyes. "Yiska."

"Yiska." She smiled. "We've already established that you're part Indian."

Papa chewed on the mouthpiece of his empty pipe, and upon hearing her comment almost choked.

"True." Yiska's expression betrayed nothing."

"Your Christian name. . ." Eliana's cheeks grew warm. "I mean, your given name. It almost sounds Jewish. Don't you think so, Papa?"

Papa shrugged.

Yiska appeared amused at her blunder. "It's Diné, Navajo."

He picked up his dented hat from the seat and fiddled with it. "It means 'after the night has passed.'"

Eliana eyed him with interest. "You're the first Navajo I've ever met. The first Indian, in fact." She directed her fingers to her chest. "My name means 'God has answered.' It's Hebrew—my mother was Jewish."

Papa tapped his pipe on his knee and stared out the window then cocked his head toward Eliana.

"Jewish?" Yiska raised his brows. "I was under the impression you were a Christian."

"Oh! Yes, we are." She let out a nervous laugh.

Yiska looked askance.

"I've adopted the Christian faith, as did my mother. Her parents died when they emigrated from Germany, and Mama met Papa shortly after that. Friends introduced them to Jesus, and I learned about Him from them." Though butterflies fluttered inside her stomach, Eliana dared to ask the next question. "Do you know much about Christianity, Yiska?"

"Some," he said. "I've heard that Jesus appeared on earth. My mother's people have never seen their gods in the flesh."

Are they his gods, too?

"Can you tell us about them?" Eliana asked.

Yiska dragged his fingers through his hair. "The Diné have many—Coyote, Water Monster, Changing Woman and her twins Monster Slayer and Child-Born-of-Water, and others. Their relationship to the sacred places—the holy lands—is more important, although they are connected."

"So many," Eliana said. "God's son, Jesus Christ, was born in the Jewish Holy Land, Israel. But that land has been taken from the Jews—it's now called Palestine. That's where my mother's ancestors were originally from."

Yiska crossed his arms. Was he thinking of all the land that had been taken away from the Indians?

The mountains rose up around them, and the coach struggled over rocks and ruts. As it ascended a steep incline, it went over a sharp swell in the road and then jerked forward. Yiska's head almost hit the ceiling. Papa's somewhat portly frame kept him situated, but Eliana nearly tumbled off her seat. *O Lord, please don't let me fall on Yiska!* Her father steadied her, and she exhaled with relief. She smoothed her skirt and tried to gather her thoughts—this conversation had its own bumps to deal with.

"Well, the important thing is that regardless of location, Jesus lives in the hearts of those who believe in Him, who turn from their sin and accept Him." Eliana placed her hand on Papa's arm. "Papa is better at explaining."

"All right." Papa leaned back in his seat and took a small pouch of tobacco from inside his coat pocket. "Allow me to present you with a word picture. Take my pipe, for example. If I fill it with tobacco and light it, it will produce smoke." He dipped the pipe into the tobacco pouch and tamped it down. Then he took a match, and with a puff ignited the fragrant hickory-scented contents.

He shook out the match and tossed it away. "By faith a believer becomes a vessel where Christ dwells—the pipe. He will smoke it, so to speak, as the believer lives out His teachings, and in turn the Christian's life produces a pleasant aroma." Papa took another puff and coughed. ". . .and a little smoker's lung, but that's beside the point. Perhaps that's a poor analogy, but it's the best I can do under the circumstances." Papa chortled.

Eliana hoped her father's example resonated with Yiska. Then, from the corner of her eye, she noticed something flicker. She glanced down. Papa's spare neckerchief had fallen to the floor. Sparks threatened to consume it.

"Papa! Your neckerchief is on fire!"

eight

Yiska stomped out the glowing edges of the neckerchief. "Safe now. Looks like your match never made it out the window."

Mr. Van Horn shook his head in disbelief.

Eliana took a deep breath. "Thank you, Yiska. Papa insists on nursing that pipe, though it's usually empty when he does so." She glanced up at her father and smiled. "But I suppose it served its purpose anyway. At least I hope it did."

"It got my attention." Yiska chuckled. "That was a good. . . picture with words. The Diné tell stories like that around their campfires." He looked at Mr. Van Horn. "Only they know how to put the fires out."

"For that you owe me a neckerchief, young man," Mr. Van Horn said with a glint in his eye. Then he leaned forward. "Yiska, what about your father?"

"My father was an Englishman. I don't know what he believed." So much of his childhood, most of his memories, remained cloaked in shadows.

"He wasn't a religious man, I take it," Van Horn said.

"I don't know. He gave thanks to the Christian God, but he also talked about the Great Spirit—mostly among the Navajo." Yiska shifted in his seat. The Van Horns listened patiently, their sincere expressions inviting him to share things that he'd hardly ever spoken.

"Pa was a mountaineer, a trader with the Navajo. He died when I was a boy, and my mother and I went back to her people. That was before The Long Walk to Fort Sumner. She sent me away to save me from that fate." Yiska swallowed hard. "She never made it back. I'd gone to live with Trask Whiley's parents, who my family knew. I helped out around his pa's trading post, and his ma taught me how to read, write, and figure."

Yiska stared at his boots for a moment then continued. "Mrs. Whiley talked about Jesus, and had me read her Bible sometimes. After the war Trask had gone out on his own. I was about sixteen when he came back. He asked me to work for him, and I've been with him ever since." Yiska sat straighter. "As far as what I believe? I'm not really sure."

&.

The stage hastened its speed. Eliana coughed as dust particles filled the air. Tension permeated the small space. *How does one respond to such a revelation?* She yearned for Yiska to embrace Christianity and would love to discuss it further, but she simply uttered a silent prayer and took comfort in knowing that Papa certainly prayed for Yiska as well.

Yiska exhaled, stared out the window for a while, then faced Eliana again. "I never did thank you for taking my photograph."

He was changing the topic of conversation. Had she offended him? Her mood plummeted.

"I didn't see that photograph," Papa said.

Eliana reached into her reticule. "I have it right here, Papa."

Her father inspected the picture. "Very good. Very good indeed. I like the way you positioned him. Suits him well. Your hat was in better shape then."

"Eh, it was," Yiska grinned. He picked up his hat and smoothed some of the dents. "It's seen better times."

"Eliana, I intended for him to keep this." Papa handed the photograph to Yiska. *Papa, no! Now how will I ever get it back?*

"Thank you, sir. She did a fine job, despite the subject." Yiska leaned back and rubbed his cheek with one of his fingers, and the corner of his mouth turned up in a crooked grin.

Eliana glanced away all flustered. *How could he?* An avalanche of thoughts assailed her—taking his picture, combing his hair, raspberry jam—and he was thinking the very same thoughts.

"Yes, and she's a good assistant. Hard worker, my girl." Papa put his hand over Eliana's. "Indeed, she's every bit as talented as I. She has a good eye."

Yiska squeezed one eye shut, and his mouth eased into a sly grin. "Which one?"

Laughter filled the coach. Yiska had such a way of putting others at ease. When they stopped laughing Eliana caught him staring at her. Was he as captivated with her as she was with him?

Papa cleared his throat, "As I was about to say, she has two pretty eyes, and a canny ability to see a good shot from behind the camera. I don't know what I'd do without her."

"Or I you, Papa." Eliana hoped she'd never have to know.

❧

Yiska stretched and loosened his bandanna. He took in a deep breath of the clean Colorado air, still feeling the ache in his ribs. The sun was high overhead. The coach had made good time on the drive to the Wagon Wheel Gap home station. Then it had taken twice as long to go the same distance to the next station, due to the rough terrain. The hotel served a hale lunch of buffalo venison stew, buttermilk biscuits, and mixed berry pie. Lucky Jim saw that the horses were changed for a fresh team.

Within half an hour they were ready to continue their course along the Rio Grande. There were no new passengers, which pleased Yiska. While Eliana and Mr. Van Horn enjoyed the view of cattle roaming the hills, Yiska enjoyed watching *her*.

"I believe that ranch belongs to Kit Carson's brother-in-law," Mr. Van Horn said. Kit Carson was responsible for sending the Navajos on their long walk. Yiska wasn't pleased at the reminder. What made him open up the way he did about his past? Did it matter that much that Eliana understand him?

Eliana glared at her father. He took her cue and changed the topic. "The stationmaster told me Wagon Wheel Gap got its name when they discovered an old wheel in the river.

They believe it was from Charles Baker's wagon when he passed through here while exploring the area."

"That's interesting, Papa. It reminds me of Mr. Snowden in Silverton, the last living member of the Baker Party." Eliana looked at Yiska. "Papa will be photographing Mr. Snowden for the *San Juan Prospector*."

Yiska wanted to ask if she would be there, too.

The Van Horns pulled out their newspapers. "Do you need some reading material, Yiska?" Eliana asked.

"No, thank you. I can't read with all this movement."

"Perhaps I could read something aloud. Would you enjoy that?"

"That sounds fine," he said.

"Oh, I know you will enjoy this!" Eliana beamed. "This is a journal entry penned by the Anonymous Explorer. The *Prospector* has been running a series of them." She began to read with a lilt in her voice.

> *A multitude of color explodes into the valley on a carpet of lush mountain meadows. Once lying dormant under the cover of winter, hearty blooms and delicate petals display their beauty and fill the air with fragrance.*
>
> *Flowers have now awakened along quiet streams and rocky places, greeting the wildlife as it enters this blissful place. This romance with nature fills my heart in a way I wonder if any human ever could.*

Though Yiska's heart raced, his face remained like stone.

Eliana sighed and folded the newspaper. "Have you ever heard such beautiful words? I can hardly imagine being surrounded by a place so sublime."

"Beautiful, yes," Yiska said. *The words are even more beautiful on your lips. How I wish I could take you there.*

"That was penned by the Anonymous Explorer." Eliana placed the paper on the seat beside her and straightened.

Mr. Van Horn raised a brow. "I wonder what place the author is describing. I'd love to go there and photograph it. Yet it seems he has kept it a secret."

"Oh, Papa, it would be wonderful to see in person!" Eliana's eyes danced.

"Any idea, Yiska?" Van Horn asked.

"It sounds like a valley west of Handies Peak. Northwest of here—in the San Juan forest between Stony Pass and Eureka Gulch."

"Have you been there?" Mr. Van Horn asked.

"Yes."

"Is it as lovely as the writer claims?" Eliana asked.

"More so."

Eliana grew quiet and looked down at her hands, and then met Yiska's eyes. "I have a confession, but please promise not to tell."

Yiska nodded.

"I found a journal on the steps at the end of the boardwalk. I brought it to the newspaper, hoping to place an ad to find the owner. But the editor decided to publish it instead."

Yiska's heart skipped a beat. "Really?"

She nodded. "I felt awful when Mr. Wilson printed it without the author's permission." She placed her hand on the newspaper. "This is art, and the work of a romantic. I hope the author is not terribly disappointed. Though I know I would have been."

"Perhaps it all worked out for the best. Mr. Van Horn, what are you reading?"

Mr. Van Horn peered up at Yiska. "*Scribner's Monthly*. An article entitled 'The Cañons of the Colorado' by Major John Wesley Powell. It's a series of three articles detailing his explorations, with engravings from Hiller's photographs. John Hiller was first hired as a boatman on the expedition, and later Powell hired him as photographer. Goes to show, if you have the ambition. . ."

Eliana leaned over her father's shoulder. "The pictures

transport you right there. That's what we. . .you. . .hope to do on the expedition, Papa." She looked at Yiska. "My father is going on a survey in New Mexico."

"He already knows about it, dear."

"Does he?" Eliana's eyes widened, filled with curiosity and alarm. "Yiska, have you been hired as the guide?"

"Well, yes, he was there when I was discussing it with Trask Whiley. And no. Yiska will not be on the expedition." Mr. Van Horn's glare issued Yiska a warning to keep silent about the matter.

Eliana looked again at the *Scribner*. "Papa, maybe your photographs will be published after the survey and circulated in a magazine."

"Sunshine, that is precisely what I hope to accomplish. Photographic documentation would not only serve to educate people, but inspire them to visit such remote places and appreciate God's creation. I would love nothing more."

Yiska's heart swelled. *Dreams so much like my own.*

"I hope you have that opportunity, Papa. And I, too, would love to see my own photographs in print. Alas, I am a woman, and that most likely shall never be." Eliana sighed.

Mr. Van Horn looked at Yiska. "What aspirations do you have, son?"

Eliana tilted her chin toward Yiska, beckoning an answer. He dared not share the nature of his dreams. He tried to disregard the rough grade beneath the wheels of the coach and the rumbling inside that cautioned him to put his growing attraction toward Eliana aside. He could tell they were pulling into the Willow Creek swing station by the slowed gait of the horses hooves.

"Whoa!" Lucky Jim hollered. The timing couldn't have been better.

🙠

The quick change of the horses at Willow Creek left Eliana feeling restless. The brief stop provided her a chance to stretch, wash her dusty face, and join the others at the well for a refreshing drink of water. In another fifteen miles, through narrow canyons and slopes, they'd arrive at Rio Grande Pass—only about three hours away, and three hours from saying farewell to Yiska.

She'd hoped she could spend more time talking with him, but a mother and her son of about eight joined them for this length of the trip. Papa assisted them as they climbed aboard and then followed. He turned to help Eliana, but Yiska took her hand and helped her up. Did he plan to ride above with Lucky Jim?

But to Eliana's delight, Yiska climbed in and sat down— beside her! She tingled all over.

"Are you an Indian?" The boy asked.

"I'm a trail guide. . .and a journalist," Yiska said.

Eliana cocked her head and eyed Yiska, mouth agape. He turned to her with a sly grin and winked. Did he mean—was Yiska the Anonymous Explorer?

The boy spoke again. "Oh. I was hoping you were an Indian." His frown of disappointment wrenched her heart.

"Why's that?" Yiska said in a gentle tone.

"I'm part Indian. And I never met a real one."

The boy's mother patted him on the knee and said in a soft voice, "Jacob, please don't bother the man."

"No bother at all, ma'am." Yiska rested his elbows on his knees and met the boy eye to eye. "Jacob, is it?"

"Yes, sir." The boy's eyes widened.

"I'm more than just an Indian, and so are you." Yiska gave a strong nod. "What do you like to do?"

"I like to build things out of wood."

Yiska grinned. "See. Jacob, the builder. I'm pleased to know you." Yiska addressed his mother. "Ma'am, you have a fine young man here."

"Thank you. Mr. . ." Were those tears the woman was blinking back?

"Wilcox. Yiska Wilcox."

"Pleased to meet you Mr. Wilcox. I am Mrs. Stafford." She

turned back to her son. "Jacob, please pull your bandanna over your mouth and nose to keep the dust out."

"But, Ma, I forgot it on the table at Grampa's cabin."

"Oh, Jacob." The boy's mother sighed and started to rummage through her satchel.

Yiska untied his neckerchief and handed it to the boy. "He can have mine."

Eliana's heart melted. *Why can't everyone see what a good man Yiska is?*

"Thank you, Mr. Wilcox." The boy took a toy soldier from his pocket and fiddled with it.

"Sure thing. And you can call me Yiska."

Eliana wondered if Jacob reminded Yiska of himself as a child. A boy looking for truth, aching to understand who he was. Similar thoughts crept into her mind about her own heritage. Why did these things matter so? Wasn't it most important simply that the child was loved? She was certain that Jacob's mother loved him. Did she remind Yiska of his own mother? Yet he was an orphan for most of his life. Eliana thought of Mama, and leaned a little closer to Papa in the seat next to her.

The stage bounced over a deep rut and tossed Eliana forward.

"Whoa." Yiska caught her and settled her back in the bench.

Eliana's face flamed as she glanced at him and let out a deep breath. "Thank you."

"Is she your wife?" Jacob asked.

"Jacob!" His mother had stretched her arm across her son's legs to keep him from bouncing about, but she yanked it back and covered her mouth.

Papa's eyes flashed open. "No, young man—she's *my* daughter. Her name is Miss Eliana, she's a photographer, and I believe she was about to take a nap. Isn't that right, dear?" Papa's lips pulled into a tight line. My, but it had been a long day.

Eliana corrected her posture and latched on to her father's arm. He rested his neck against the back cushion and nodded off as the coach rattled along. Yiska leaned back and pulled his hat down over his eyes. Jacob was soon asleep with his head against his mother's arm. Eliana smiled at Mrs. Stafford, wishing they could have some female conversation, but found herself settling against Papa's shoulder.

As her eyes fluttered shut she became more aware of Yiska's presence beside her—the warmth of his leg radiating to hers through her skirts, his muscular arm burrowed against hers, his shallow breathing. Out of the corner of her eye, she saw Yiska tilt his hat and steal a peek at her, but she chose to ignore it. A myriad of thoughts rolled into her mind. Was it wise for her to be this close to him with the feelings she was starting to have? There was still so much she did not know about him. Eliana's swirling thoughts and the rhythm of the coach lulled her to sleep.

A burst of noise jarred the passengers awake. Shots rang out, and the horses bolted. Jacob's mother screamed and flung herself down on the seat to cover her son.

nine

"Everybody down!" Adrenaline surged through Yiska's body at the sound of gunfire. A strong instinct to protect Eliana overcame him, but her father's shielding arms thwarted his effort.

The coach sped up, and he reached across the floorboards to retrieve his rifle from under the seat. Jacob's mother peeked up at Yiska, her eyes full of fright. The boy didn't appear harmed. Mr. Van Horn had found his own rifle and was readying the gun. Yiska peered out the windows on each side to assess the situation. Who was out there? Bandits? Utes?

Shots resounded. Yiska and Mr. Van Horn fired back. A bullet thwacked against the coach. They returned more fire.

"Ma, you're bleeding," Jacob cried. Blood seeped through her sleeve.

Eliana crouched down next to the boy's mother and tried to steady herself on the bouncing floorboards. She pushed the woman's sleeve back farther to try to examine the wound, but the task was impossible during the chase. At least the blood wasn't gushing. That must be a good sign.

She tore off a piece of her petticoat, pressed it against the wound, and wrapped her other arm around the terrified woman's shoulders. "I think it only grazed her arm, Jacob. She'll be all right."

The gunfire subsided. Had the culprits retreated? The coach pitched over bumps and ruts, its speed increasing. Yiska clutched the edge of the seat. Something was very wrong. Was Lucky Jim down? He shouted to Mr. Van Horn. "I think the horses are running on their own. I'm going up."

"Yiska." The concern in Eliana's voice pricked his pounding heart. His desire to protect her overwhelmed him,

73

but they might crash if he didn't do something. Then he remembered—her father had called her Eagle Eye Eli.

"Cover me." He handed her his rifle, and she positioned herself near the window and cocked it.

Yiska hauled himself up to the window's ledge and grabbed hold of the rails above. The wind whipped him, and he clamped his hat tighter.

Another shot echoed. Eliana and Van Horn fired back. Yiska pulled himself on top of the rocking coach and lay on his belly.

He cupped his hands around his mouth and shouted. "Eliana, my rifle." She handed it up to him.

He crawled forward to the driver's box. Lucky Jim slumped on the footboard, the reins caught under his arm. Yiska bent to grab them, and another shot whizzed over his head. He raised his rifle and fired back. Four Utes had come out of hiding, whooping and hollering on horseback as they circled the careening coach. The renegades reared their horses and shot their guns into the air. They left in a flash, their horses kicking up dirt in their wake.

Yiska wedged his gun between his legs. Sweat soaked his brow as he grabbed hold of the reins, and tried to gain control of the runaway team. The spooked horses ran wild over rocks and ruts, rattling the stage like the rumble of an avalanche. Dust filled the air, blinding Yiska's view. He held the reins firmly, but tried to give them enough slack so the horses could guide themselves on instinct—any abrupt turns could tip the coach onto its side. He hoped the wheels of the vehicle were as sturdy as they looked. If he could only get the horses to settle into a normal gait, he might be able to bring them to a stop.

"Yiska," Lucky Jim groaned.

Yiska startled. He'd thought Lucky Jim was dead. Relief eased some of his tension.

"Pull the brake, slowly. The resistance will signal them to stop."

"I'm trying. A branch is stuck in there."

Jim stirred, clamping one hand to his bloody shoulder. "Give me the reins and get it out."

"You sure?"

"If you don't get that brake loose, the horses are going to go right down into that ravine around the bend—and all of us with them."

Yiska gripped underneath the seat and leaned forward. The rutted road sped by beneath him. The pounding of the horses' hooves filled his ears. He gritted his teeth, reached down, and pulled on the tree limb that was wedged against the brake.

It didn't budge.

He fumbled for the hatchet and whacked at the branch, careful not to slice into the brake. At last it broke free and flew downwind. Now he could control the lever. He gripped the metal handle and pulled back, gently at first, then exerting more pressure. Jim propped himself up and gritted his teeth while he pulled on the reins.

The stagecoach slowed its pace, and with the resistance the horses' terror waned. Soon they slowed to a trot. Lucky Jim handed Yiska the reins. "Pull 'em in now. Easy does it."

"Whoaaaa." Yiska pulled back on the reins, increasing the tension against the bits. The hitch chains jangled as the four-in-hand team came to a complete stop, this time with no hostlers to come out to greet them.

"Now lock the brake," Lucky Jim said.

Yiska secured the coach and scanned the timbered foothills that bordered the rugged trail. No sign of their pursuers. He exhaled, muscles relaxing, and hollered down to the passengers. "All's clear. You can come out now, with caution."

❧

Eliana disembarked, shaken by the tumultuous ride. Papa helped her down with rifle still in hand. He also offered his hand to help Mrs. Stafford and reassured her son that she would be all right.

After the coach slowed, Eliana had managed to tie her scrap of petticoat around the woman's arm as a makeshift bandage. If no infection set in, the wound would heal in no time.

"Are you all right, Sunshine?" Papa asked.

Eliana threw her arms around him. A lump formed in her throat. "Yes, Papa. Are you?"

Papa wiped the dirt and sweat from his brow. "It takes a lot more than a little gunfire to upset me."

Anxious to see Yiska, Eliana hurried to the front of the coach where the horses stood, soaked and lathered.

He looked down at her from the driver's seat, a slow grin easing onto his dusty face.

Her eyes moistened. "Are you all right?"

"Yes." He wiped his face with the back of his hand.

Papa walked up beside her. "And what about the driver?"

"Lucky Jim was shot in the shoulder. Help me get him down," Yiska said. "We're still a couple hours from the next station, and his wound needs tending."

The two men helped Lucky Jim down and got him into the coach. Young Jacob held the door open to allow fresh air inside. Eliana ripped more of her petticoat for bandages and climbed inside to take care of Jim. Jacob's mother, though a little pale, waited outside, resting on a boulder with a watchful eye on her son while Papa stood guard.

"You saved us," Jacob said. His wide eyes, full of admiration, looked up at Yiska.

"Well, I had a little help." Yiska turned toward Eliana, his gaze resting on her face.

Something about the way Yiska looked at her made her feel more connected to him with each passing moment. Each experience they went through together brought them closer, strengthening a bond she couldn't understand. Yet, as with an undeveloped photograph, she still could not envision what might yet come.

"Miss Eliana can sure shoot a gun," Jacob said.

"Yes, she can," Papa said.

"Thank you for watching my back." Yiska turned and nodded at Jacob. "The Van Horns make a good team."

He poked his head inside the coach. "How is he?"

"Ask me yourself—I'm not dead," said Lucky Jim. Eliana held back a giggle.

Yiska lifted his chin. "Now I know how you got your name."

"Luck ain't got nothin' to do with it. The good Lord has been watchin' out for me for a long time. Matter o' fact, He was watching out for all of us today."

Jacob piped up. "He was. I know it!"

"How's that, Jacob?" Yiska asked.

"I was praying to Him the whole time. He even heard me over all that shootin'!"

Everyone started to laugh and Eliana's heart warmed. *Out of the mouths of babes.* Perhaps Yiska would see God's hand in his life. *Thank You, heavenly Father.*

"Yiska, are you going to drive the stage to the next station?" Jacob asked. "I'll ride shotgun."

"Oh, no you won't, young man," his mother said.

Yiska ruffled Jacob's hair. "I'll tell you what, you can help me check the horses."

"Sure," Jacob said. "Hey, Yiska. Who was shootin' at us? Indians?"

Yiska looked from Jacob to Lucky Jim. "They appeared to be Utes. Probably just trying to stir up trouble."

Lucky Jim touched his bandages. "Thank you, Miss Van Horn. I'll be getting along now."

Eliana gave Lucky Jim a scolding look. "But you've just been shot. You need to ride back here so you can rest." She checked to see that he wasn't bleeding through his bandages.

"I won't get any rest unless I'm up on the driver's box, miss." Lucky Jim groaned as he sat up. "Yiska, I'm going to need some help up there. You make a fine jehu."

Yiska helped Jim out of the coach then leaned back in. He

took Eliana's hand and squeezed it, and then he left. Warmth spread through her veins like a gentle stream that nourished the blossoms in a hidden valley.

⁂

Yiska gazed at Eliana as she relaxed in a wooden rocker on the front porch of the log cabin. The building served as the hotel and restaurant for the Rio Grande Pass home station. After the attack, it took them two long hours to get here, fourteen from the time the stage pulled out of Del Norte that morning. It was good to be able to stop for the night in this serene valley. The stationmaster wouldn't have a replacement driver coming in until the morning, and everyone seemed grateful for the reprieve.

A satisfying meal of fried pork, potatoes, gravy, bread, and custard pie had left him feeling quite subdued. As Eliana sat reading, loose tendrils of hair spilled down around her face like a waterfall. The last rays of sun illuminated golden highlights.

She looked up and smiled. "I didn't see you there."

"I didn't want to bother you," Yiska said.

"You're not. Please, sit down."

Yiska eyed the Bible on her lap. "What are you reading?"

"Psalm 138." Eliana looked down and read from the open page, her voice soothing to his ear. "'I will praise thee with my whole heart: before the gods will I sing praise unto thee. I will worship toward thy holy temple, and praise thy name for thy lovingkindness and for thy truth: for thou hast magnified thy word above all thy name. In the day when I cried thou answeredst me, and strengthenedst me with strength in my soul.'" She placed her hand on the page and glanced up at Yiska.

He answered me today. The thought entered Yiska's mind like an echo calling across a canyon. He looked at the Bible with interest. "That book is important to you."

"Mm. It's life to me," Eliana said. "It belonged to my mother. Papa and I usually read from it after dinner, but tonight his head was throbbing, so I encouraged him to retire early. Maria and Jacob have turned in as well."

"Maria?" Yiska squinted.

"Mrs. Stafford, Jacob's mother. Come to find out, she's my friend Celia's older sister, whom I had never met. They'll travel on to Lake City with us tomorrow." Eliana smiled. "Maria was hurting some from her injury, and she and Jacob were both exhausted."

"It was a brutal day." Yiska shook his head. "I checked on Lucky Jim. One of the stable hands helped the stationmaster remove the bullet. He thinks Jim will be all right. Said you did a good job tending his wound."

"It wasn't the first time. Papa and I have encountered other unfortunate incidents out here."

"I take it this wasn't the first time you ever handled a rifle," Yiska said.

"No. . .but you seemed to know that," Eliana said.

"I guess I overheard something recently about Eagle Eye Eli."

Eliana's face turned as many shades of pink as the color hiding behind the clouds in the evening sky—only she had nowhere to hide.

She buried her face in her hands and shook her head. "I can't believe it. You know I. . . ?"

Yiska smirked. "Yes. . .size small men's dungarees."

"But you do know. . ."

"That you wear the disguise for protection?"

"Yes. And that I'm. . ."

"Going on the expedition with your father."

Eliana threw her head back and moaned. "Why would he tell you?"

"He didn't. I heard him discussing the expedition with Mr. Whiley."

"Mr. Whiley is the only other one who knows. The disguise was a plan to keep me safe when I assist Papa." She rolled her eyes. "You, of all people, had to find out. Did you suspect it when we were at the mercantile?"

"I already knew."

Eliana exhaled deeply. "Well, you might as well tell me. What did my father say when he learned that you knew about it?"

"He and Mr. Whiley discussed it. They decided that it would be unsafe for me to go on the expedition as the guide. They thought I'd give you away. Something about. . .the way I look at you." Yiska had argued the point with them to no avail. *Could it be that obvious?*

The corner of her mouth curved. "You're the guide for the Robbins survey?"

"Was."

Yiska stood and scanned the horizon then turned back to Eliana. "The sun will be down soon. I need to go check on Shadow. He's out in the pasture." He extended his hand toward her. "Come with me."

She stood and placed her hand in his. So delicate and soft. He held it until they'd descended the front steps. Despite the wearisome day, she still looked lovely. Her dark green dress sprinkled with tiny flowers reminded him of a certain valley. *Beautiful.*

"Will you be cold?" he asked.

Eliana adjusted her shawl. "No. This will be fine."

As they made their way toward the pasture, a majestic view of the Rio Grande opened before them. A clearing in a grove of ponderosa pines revealed the winding river below and the sun setting in the distance behind mountains tipped in white.

"How lovely. It's hard to imagine that there are so many wonderful places in the Territory."

"But there are." *And I wish to show you all of them.*

Eliana tilted her head. "You should know, Mr. Anonymous Explorer." A satisfied grin crept across her lips.

Yiska shrugged. "Looks like *my* secret is out, too."

She lowered her lashes then looked up with misty eyes. "I feel awful. I almost ruined everything for you. Your plans. Your dreams."

Eliana. You are my plans. My dreams. He lifted her chin with the tip of his finger and gazed into the deep pools of her eyes. "Everything worked out fine. I have an assignment to interview Mr. Snowden in Silverton? And if I have my facts straight, there's a certain photography assistant that I might get to see there."

Her countenance softened. Was it relief? Expectation? "Now, shhh." He wanted to take her in his arms but resisted. He could almost see the reflection of the sunset in her eyes. "It will be getting dark soon." He took her hand, and they approached a split rail fence. He let out a sharp whistle, and Shadow appeared from a dusky corner of the pasture, galloping toward him.

Black as midnight, Shadow pranced around, shaking his head up and down. He came up to the fence and nuzzled Yiska's face. Yiska caressed his nose and then put his arm around the horse's head and patted his muscular neck. "Shadow, my friend. Looks like they treated you well."

Eliana smiled. "He's a handsome horse. No wonder you're proud of him."

Yiska's smile widened. "I couldn't ask for a better one." He climbed over the fence to check Shadow over. He slid his hand over the mustang's sleek coat and down his legs, inspecting every inch of him.

"How'd you come by him?"

Yiska looked up at Eliana. "He was wild. A rancher up in Gunnison helped me train him." Yiska patted Shadow's haunch. "Well, Shadow, looks like you'll be ready to hit the trail tomorrow morning."

Eliana's face fell. Was she as disappointed as he that tomorrow their paths would take new directions?

"We ought to get back before it's too dark," she said.

"Have you forgotten that I am a guide?" Yiska asked, as they turned back toward the cabin.

" 'Tis true. . .*and* a journalist."

"And a journalist. Thanks to you." Yiska smiled. "When

do you expect to be in Silverton? Perhaps I could meet you there."

Eliana's eyes brightened. "Yes. You could conduct your interview, and then we could take the photograph."

"A good idea... But I would like to see *you* again, Eliana."

"The one who's responsible for you not getting to go on the survey?"

"The very one." Yiska gazed into her eyes. "I can't help the way I look at you."

"The way you're looking at me now?" She tilted her chin and flashed her dancing eyes at him. "Or perhaps the way you looked at me as I saw you through the lens when I took your photograph. There *was* a certain look you had that day... a stifled smile perhaps?"

"Can I help it if you make me smile?"

"That reminds me. You have something that belongs to me."

Yiska thought of the ribbon he had bought for her. How did she know?

She raised her eyebrows. "The picture of you that my father confiscated. It belongs to me, you know. It was a fair trade."

"Ah, but it was given back to me, so now it's mine." A grin eased across Yiska's face. "I'm willing to trade."

"For what?" The look in Eliana's eyes dared him to suggest a worthy exchange.

"For this." Yiska caressed her face with his fingers and with a gentle touch lifted her chin. As he looked into her warm eyes, he sensed her timidity. "Have you never kissed an Indian?"

"No... I have never kissed any man."

Yiska enveloped her in his arms and pressed his lips against hers, savoring her sweetness beneath the twilight sky.

☙

Eliana awoke with a start, and her eyes scanned the small, unfamiliar room. The relay station was nothing more than a large log cabin; her bed, a small cot. The room was sparse, with only a washbasin sitting upon a pedestal table and a single chair against the wall—her shawl draped on it—and a horseshoe wedged above the doorframe, for luck.

She jumped to her feet and looked down at her wrinkled dress. When had she fallen asleep? She hardly remembered coming back to the station last night. She was utterly exhausted after the long ride on the stagecoach yesterday. And blessed. They had all been in grave danger. *Thank You for a new day, heavenly Father, and please bring quick healing to Lucky Jim and Maria.*

She rubbed her arms in the morning chill. Thoughts of her time with Yiska the evening before swept over her with warmth. Had he really kissed her? She closed her eyes, and images of his tawny skin, his dark hair, and enchanting eyes looking deep into her own sent a tingle over her skin. She could almost feel his touch. His closeness. She reached for her shawl and recalled how he had wrapped his buckskin coat around her on their way back to the cabin. As she draped the shawl around herself, she imagined the warmth and scent of leather. And of him.

She searched for her reticule to retrieve her comb and make herself presentable before going downstairs. She hoped she would see him again before he left.

She remembered that she'd placed her small bag in Papa's room for safekeeping. As she hurried across the landing to his room, the smell of bacon and fresh-baked bread filled her senses. The stationmaster's wife met her in the hallway.

"Good mornin'. You're in a hurry today."

"Yes, good morning." Eliana saw that the woman held her mother's Bible.

"I was asked to see that you got this. Apparently you left it on the porch last night."

"Oh, thank you." Eliana smiled and took a step forward, eager to be on her way so she could get downstairs.

The woman touched her arm. "That young fella, Yiska, gave it to me before he rode out. Said it was important that you get it."

Eliana turned, her heart sinking. "He's gone?"

"Yes, miss. Pulled out before the sun was up. My husband told him about some men who were in need of a guide." The woman put her hands in her apron pockets and gave Eliana a knowing smile. "Breakfast will be served shortly."

The stationmaster's wife walked away, leaving her alone in the hall. Eliana hugged the Bible and sighed. *Lord, would it be Your will for me to see him again?*

She looked down at the Bible and opened the cover. There inside lay the cabinet card photograph of Yiska. He had returned it. Hope and longing filled her heart. She closed her eyes to hold back the flood of tears that threatened to release.

"There you are." Papa appeared at the top of the stairs, a glint in his eye. "Are you ready, Sunshine? Our journey awaits."

ten

Lake City, Colorado

"It's a miracle that our cargo made it here in one piece," Eliana said as she and her father sorted through the new photography equipment and supplies in the back room of their studio. The small shop was almost a second home to them, as quaint as their clapboard house situated next door.

Papa inspected his new camera with a critical eye. "I was more than a bit worried for a while, but the good Lord saw fit to keep everything intact."

"And us, too." Eliana kissed him on the cheek.

"We won't make any new appointments while we're here, unless it's something important. We already have enough work to keep us busy until we head out again."

Eliana picked up a small carton from the floor and placed it on the counter. "You do remember that Celia is coming in next Monday for her wedding portraits? I still can't believe she's getting married." Eliana glanced up. "I thought she would be one of the last among my friends to settle down—she's so particular. But Thomas won her heart." Eliana sighed.

"Seems rather rushed to me," Papa said.

"The preacher, Reverend George Darley, is coming to town. And if the weather is nice, they'll be married out at Lake San Cristobal."

"How you gathered all this news already mystifies me. We haven't even been back a full day." Papa grinned. "Hand me that cloth, please." Papa carefully wiped the lenses. "You know, Sunshine, one of these days I suppose you'll marry, too. Your mother warned me of such a thing, but I never wanted

85

to believe it. You've become a remarkable young woman before my very eyes."

"It's not as if I'm available for courting. Most of my time is spent behind the camera or in men's clothing. Or both." Eliana shook her head. "It's hard to get a gentleman to notice you that way."

Papa rubbed his whiskers. "Well, I seem to know a young man who's taken notice of you."

Was he displeased? She would ignore the comment. Eliana finished inspecting the thin iron plates. "All of the plates are in fine condition. Now we'll need to blacken them, and then we can pack them up for the expedition."

"I'll japan them myself," Papa said. "I wrote out a list of tasks for you this morning. Now, back to the subject at hand."

"I don't know what you mean. . .unless perhaps you're speaking of Cornelius Crawford?" Eliana laughed. "He's not even my type."

Papa chuckled. "You know whom I'm speaking of, dear."

Eliana lowered her lashes. "I may never see him again."

"If my suspicions are correct, he'll find his way to you somehow."

Oh, how she hoped.

❧

Yiska pulled open the flap of his saddlebag to retrieve his journal and a pencil. This would make a good spot to get some rest and do some writing. The pool of water would provide refreshment for both him and Shadow, and the shade would feel good after riding in the bright sun for most of the day. A little jerky and dried fruit would do for now to curb his hunger, and later he would try to catch some trout.

He sat down on a large rock by the stream. Water flowed into it from a precipice above. Dappled sunlight filtered through the trees, and visions of Eliana's sweet face, her clear hazel eyes, the slight dimple in her chin, and her adorable smile filled him with wonder. Eliana Van Horn disturbed his thoughts, challenged his beliefs, and filled the long-vacant crevices of his heart.

Yiska untied the cord that bound his journal and opened it. From between the pages, he pulled out the photograph of the beautiful woman who had changed his life forever. He'd never given any credence to the idea of sharing his life with someone, yet now she seemed to be the compass navigating his every thought.

He would see her again. Perhaps not on the expedition, and it may not be in Silverton, but he would track her back to Lake City if he had to, just to hold her once again.

❧

Eliana displayed Celia and Thomas's wedding photographs on a table covered with a white linen cloth. She admired how well they had come out—the family sitting and bridal portraits were stunning. But the one with Celia standing behind her soon-to-be groom was Eliana's favorite. Celia wore a beautiful new paisley shawl, which she would someday use for her child's christening.

Eliana imagined how the couple's children and grandchildren would enjoy the pictures and ruminate over their happiness on this occasion, as she treasured the daguerreotype of her own parents' wedding. How lovely Mama looked, and Papa, so proud and handsome. Perhaps she would marry, too, someday, though her heart ached knowing that Momma would not be there to share her joy. How she longed for conversation that only a mother and daughter could share, especially now, when her heart overflowed with so many new feelings. So many thoughts of Yiska.

"These photographs came out lovely, Eliana. Celia will be pleased." Maria Stafford leaned over the table to admire the pictures of her sister's wedding party.

"Oh! Maria, you startled me. Thank you for saying so." Eliana smiled at her new friend. "This family portrait with you in it came out very nice. You photograph very well. I'd love to take a picture of you and Jacob sometime."

"I'm sure Jacob would like that. You've already done so

much. It's nice to have a place of our own again after living for such a long time with others. It was very kind of your father to let the upstairs apartment to us."

"I'm glad it pleases you. Why don't you have some tea with me? I was about to take a break."

A short time later, the women sat in wicker chairs on the side porch of the studio, enjoying their tea and the pleasant afternoon.

Maria took a sip and placed her cup back on the saucer. "Where will you be traveling, Eliana?"

"Papa and I have to photograph some of the mining areas, and then we have a special assignment to photograph a prominent citizen in Silverton. It will accompany an interview to be published in the *San Juan Prospector*."

"Your travels sound exciting, but I do hope you are careful." Maria arched an eyebrow. "Although you are rather skilled at handling dangerous situations. Thank you again for helping me with my injury."

"How is your wound?" Eliana took a sip from her porcelain cup.

"It's healing well, thank you." Maria massaged her arm. "It seems like I've been healing in one way or another for over a year now. Losing my husband in a mining accident was more painful than any bullet wound could ever be. But I'm doing much better now and have become stronger for it." Maria took another sip of her tea.

"It must've been very difficult for you," Eliana said. "There are many risks in loving someone, are there not?"

"Do you speak of Yiska?" Maria asked. "I've noticed something special between the two of you."

Eliana felt the roses bloom in her cheeks. "Is it that obvious?"

"Well, Jacob seemed to notice." Maria gave her a gentle smile. "Love cannot be hidden. It even shines in the darkest places. Look at Celia and Thomas—when he became gravely ill this spring, it made her realize how true her feelings for him were. He insists it was her love that pulled him through."

"Yes, but is love enough?" Eliana asked.

"No, it isn't. You must also have faith," Maria said. "In God, and each other."

The two women sat in silence, pondering these thoughts. As Eliana stared at the porch floor, a large boot landed on one of the steps. She glanced up, surprised to see Trask Whiley.

"Good afternoon, ladies." Mr. Whiley flashed a wide grin.

"Mr. Whiley! What brings you to Lake City?" Eliana greeted him with a cheerful smile, despite her reservations about his not allowing Yiska to go on the survey.

"I had some business up this way. Just arrived on the Southern Overland Express. Perhaps I should've traveled here with you and your father last week," he said.

Eliana and Maria looked at one another then shook their heads with utmost dismay.

"No. That would not have been a good idea," Eliana said. "We encountered some trouble on the way."

"Yes," Maria said, "but we had a heroic young man with us who saved us from marauding Indians." She glanced at Eliana and smiled.

"Yiska." Mr. Whiley said.

"You know him?" Maria asked.

"Yes. I'm his boss. . .and his friend. Was anyone wounded?"

"The driver was shot in the shoulder. . .and a bullet grazed Mrs. Stafford's arm."

Mr. Whiley's eyes widened, and he shook his head. "I'm sorry to hear that, ma'am."

Maria nodded. "Thank you. I'm recovering quite well and am thankful no one was seriously injured."

"Forgive me, I've neglected to introduce you," Eliana said. "This is Mrs. Maria Stafford. She and her son rent the apartment above our studio. They moved here from Willow Creek."

"That's down my way, more or less." Mr. Whiley tipped his

hat. "Mrs. Stafford, a pleasure."

"Ma, Ma!" Jacob ran up and threw his arms around his mother's neck. "Can I go down to the creek? Ace's pa is going to take us fishing."

"Sure, son, but please mind your manners and say hello to Mr. Whiley, a friend of the Van Horns and of Yiska's."

"Howdy, sir. You know Yiska? He's my friend, too. He saved our lives!" Jacob smiled up at the tall man.

"That's what I've heard." Mr. Whiley grinned. "Any good fish in that creek?"

"Ace said it's filled with trout. You can come with us if you'd like."

Mr. Whiley chuckled. "Maybe another day. I have some things I need to take care of. By the way, Miss Van Horn, where can I find your father?"

"He's out for the remainder of the afternoon, but you can see him at dinner tonight. That is, if you'll come. We'll eat at five o'clock. Maria and Jacob will be joining us."

"Five o'clock then. Ladies. Jacob." Mr. Whiley tilted his hat and sauntered away.

Maria turned to Eliana and whispered, "I didn't know we are invited to dinner this evening."

"You are now. But I'll need your help cooking the meal. I'm much better behind a camera than behind a stove."

≈

"Easy there, Shadow." Yiska leaned back as he led his horse down a rocky crag. He had escorted a small convoy of miners to Cunningham Gulch and now was headed back through Stony Pass. The anxious men he'd guided hoped to strike a silver vein in the hard-to-reach area and somehow managed to haul along some large, steam-powered equipment and other supplies with the help of their burros.

Yiska continued his trek northeast and hoped to arrive at Rose's Cabin within a few days. Miners who flooded the area almost always kept the new building's many rooms occupied. Mr. Whiley had arranged for Yiska to use this stop as a connecting point for his next assignment. On his way there, he would go through the valley that had enthralled Eliana. Though it wouldn't be as colorful as he'd described until after the summer rains, it would provide easier terrain for him and Shadow.

☙

Eliana marveled at the picturesque setting of Lake San Cristobal as friends and family gathered to celebrate Celia and Thomas's wedding. Mountain views surrounded them, and pines towered over them, providing the perfect amount of shade. The wedding couldn't have taken place on a finer day.

Eliana, in her new blue dress, swirled around with Papa to the gleeful sound of fiddles.

"You're a fine dancer, Papa," she said.

Papa's eyes crinkled. "As are you, my Sunshine. I'm going to sit this next one out, but I think I see someone who can take my place." Papa snagged Jacob's arm as he passed by. "Would you do me a favor, young man, and dance with Miss Eliana?"

"Sure, Mr. Van Horn. I won't be dancing with Ma anymore, since Mr. Whiley finally got her to dance with him," Jacob said.

The fiddles started to play again. Eliana took Jacob's hands, and they swung round and round until the music stopped. "Thank you for the dance, sir." She tried to catch her breath.

"I'm going to get some lemonade. Would you like some, Miss Eliana?" Jacob asked.

"That sounds like a grand idea, thank you. Would you bring it to me over at our picnic blanket?"

"Sure. I'll get some cake, too."

"Didn't I already see you with some cake?" Eliana asked.

An impish grin appeared on Jacob's face. "Maybe."

"Well, I won't tell," Eliana whispered.

She made her way to the old patchwork quilt that was spread out under a large pine. Papa leaned up against the tree talking with Reverend Darley, the minister who had performed the nuptials.

"It's such a beautiful day for a wedding!" Eliana beamed. "Reverend Darley, Celia was pleased that you were here to perform the ceremony."

"It was my pleasure. And although this is a grand place for a wedding, maybe by this time next year others will have the privilege of having theirs in a church," Reverend Darley said.

"A church in Lake City? How wonderful."

"My brother, Alexander, the other Reverend Darley, is planning to start one here. He's a carpenter as well as a minister, and he intends to build it himself."

"Excellent! I'm sure many will support the effort," Papa said.

"And what about you, Reverend Darley?" Eliana asked.

"I'm pioneering in the San Juans. My mission is to bring the Gospel to the western slope. There are many new settlements and mining towns that need to hear the Word of God. There are some who haven't heard it since they arrived here. I've preached to men, women, and burros, alike." Reverend Darley smiled, arms resting across his knees.

Eliana tilted her chin. "If there are no churches, where do you preach?"

Reverend Darley held his hands out. "Anywhere they'll listen. I'll sit down with them in the mining camps or call a meeting in a saloon. I meet them where they are, as the Lord does with us."

"It sounds like you're a missionary," Eliana said.

He nodded. "I am. Are not all believers bearing witness to Christ wherever they go?"

Eliana thought about that. There was much truth in what he said.

"Since we are made in His image, I suppose we ought to reflect Him to others. Aye?"

Eliana turned to Papa. "That reminds me of Reverend Mattheson and his enthusiasm for telling others about the Lord."

"Do you mean Harland Mattheson?" Reverend Darley asked. "I believe he is occupied as a naturalist now. Does some work for the government."

Eliana looked at her father in confusion then turned back to Reverend Darley. "Isn't he preaching anymore?"

"Oh, I don't think we've heard his last sermon yet."

Maria and Mr. Whiley walked over, lemonade in hand. Maria sat down on the blanket beside Eliana, but Mr. Whiley remained standing, towering above them like one of the ponderosa pines.

Papa turned to the minister. "Reverend Darley, you've met Mrs. Stafford, Celia's sister. And this is a friend of ours, Trask Whiley, here on business from Del Norte."

Reverend Darley cocked his head. "Del Norte, eh? Gateway to the San Juans. What type of business are you here for, Mr. Whiley?"

"I own an outfitting company and thought I'd investigate the possibility of opening another in Lake City."

Jacob ran up to Eliana, a cup of lemonade sloshing about, and handed it to her, along with a plate of wedding cake. "Here, Miss Eliana."

"Thank you, Jacob. You're a true gentleman."

Reverend Darley looked directly at Mr. Whiley. "You know, I'm about the Lord's business, and I'd be pleased if you'd join us for Sunday meeting tomorrow. I've called a service at the grange. The ladies will pack baskets, and a hymn sing will follow."

Jacob tugged Mr. Whiley's arm, "You won't miss it, Mr. Whiley, will you?"

Mr. Whiley looked down at Jacob, "I suppose it wouldn't hurt any." He glanced at Maria. "You'll be there, I take it?" Now it was Maria's turn to blush.

In a flash, Jacob ran off again to play with some cousins.

Mr. Whiley addressed Papa. "John, about that business we discussed a few nights ago. I've decided to send Yiska on the survey after all. I think it would be in everyone's best interest." Mr. Whiley glanced at Eliana. "The benefits outweigh the risks."

"I've given it some thought myself and am in full agreement," Papa said.

Elated, Eliana refrained from hugging Papa.

"If everything works out," Whiley said, "he'll have an additional role other than being a guide. I got word this morning that editor Wilson at the *Prospector* wants to hire him as a correspondent for the survey."

"What a great opportunity. It's not a conflict for you?" Papa asked.

"Not at all. In fact, I've been hoping he'd get a break like that. It will be good for him."

Maria looked up at Mr. Whiley. "Yiska mentioned that he was a journalist. If he's half as good as that Anonymous Explorer I've read lately, he's bound to make a name for himself." Mr. Whiley, Papa, and Eliana smiled knowingly at one another.

"Did I miss something?" she asked. At that moment, Jacob appeared by his mother's side, faced flushed from play. "Oh, mercy, look at you. I might have to walk you down to the lake and let you have a swim."

Eliana's heart filled with joy for Yiska' good news. She would get to see him again! Her heart raced. She told herself to breathe lest she swoon from all the excitement.

"Mr. Whiley, how do you plan on letting him know?" she asked.

"If I only had a way to get word to him along the trail, maybe at Rose's Cabin, but I can't get out there myself."

"Maybe I could be of assistance," Reverend Darley said. "I'm traveling that way and will be there for a couple of days. Then I'll head down to Silverton as well. Chances are I'll run into the fellow. What did you say his name is?"

"Yiska." Jacob piped up. "He's part Indian, but that's not all he is. He's a journalist, too!"

As the adults laughed, Eliana dared to hope. Could it be

that Yiska's dreams would soon come true? And could they ever include her? *Lord, please watch over Yiska, wherever he may be.*

❧

Yiska led Shadow along a narrow path high on a ridge. Mountain walls rose around him, but soon a green valley would be in view, dotted with rocks and streams and colored with purple lupine, red prairie fire, and blue columbine.

As he turned the corner he came upon a pair of yearling brown bears about ten yards in front of him. He laid a hand on Shadow's neck, careful not to make any abrupt moves. "Steady, boy," he whispered.

As the bears came closer he reached for the rifle that hung from his saddle and scanned the area. One of the bears swiped at the other, and a playful wrestling match ensued. Shadow snorted and began to back away. The young bears looked up.

Yiska dropped the reins and cocked his gun, his heart thumping in his chest. The yearlings scampered away. Barely breathing, he waited before resuming his journey. Was the mother bear nearby?

He listened, surrounded by mountain stillness and the sigh of the wind through the pines. Exhaling in relief, he lowered his gun, gathered the reins, and rubbed Shadow's crest to calm him. Shadow pawed the ground, agitated, and attempted to turn.

The yearlings' mother charged toward them, a brown blur on the path. Yiska jerked his rifle up and fired. The she bear leaped for Yiska. She slammed into Shadow's flank then fell dead.

Shadow reared back from the bear's massive weight, neighing shrilly. Yiska scrambled for the reins and flew backward over the edge of the ridge.

He landed on a ledge several yards below in a motionless heap.

eleven

Yiska moaned as he awoke to the damp nudge of Shadow's nose against his face. The horse's reins dangled on the ground. As his vision cleared, he realized he'd fallen from the narrow ridge above. How his horse found his way down and across the wide ledge he didn't question—Shadow's instincts were far better than his own.

Yiska pulled himself up and looked down over the ledge. His rifle lay broken on the boulders below. He felt his hip for his side arm and was glad it was still there. He rubbed his sides and let out a slow exhale. His ribs were still intact. Except for some aches and bruises, he was all right. He sat up and grabbed his canteen from the pack behind his saddle, took a swig, and splashed a bit on his face.

Yiska made his way back up the ridge, Shadow in tow. There lay the lifeless four-hundred-pound bear. He took off his coat and shirt and laid them on a rock. He tossed his hat there with them and wrapped a headband around his brow to keep his hair out of his face. He'd salvage the bear skin and whatever meat he could take with him. Nature would dispose of the refuse, but he'd have to work fast before the scent of blood drew the attention of wildcats or coyotes. He kneeled over the animal, preparing to cut away its thick coat.

Click.

Yiska looked up, sun glinting in his eyes. The barrel of a shotgun stared him in the face.

"I hope you intend to share that with me, Injun." A weather-beaten man in fringed buckskins and a wide-brimmed hat glared at him.

Yiska eyed him carefully. He kept his voice calm. "Put that gun away, and I'll give you what you want. There's plenty

96

here, but I could use a hand."

The heavily bearded man lowered his shotgun. "My name's Bouclier—they call me Buck."

"Yiska Wilcox."

"You Whiley's scout?"

"I am."

Buck eyed the bear. "Looks like ya got yerself a good-sized brownie."

"She almost got me," Yiska said. "I'll take as much as I can, and you can have the rest."

"What are you planning to do with the fur?" the man asked.

Yiska stood. "I might trade it up at Rose's Cabin."

The mountaineer hoisted his shotgun back over his shoulder. "I could take it off yer hands. . .for a fair trade." The man pointed his chin toward his horse and a fully loaded pack mule.

Yiska swatted a fly away from his face. "Lost my rifle over the edge of that ridge."

"Good then. Let's get to work on that beast."

The task complete, Yiska washed the thick, red blood from his arms and chest while Shadow drank from the stream. He cleaned his hatchet and knife and dried them with a bandanna. He strapped huge portions of meat wrapped in oilcloth behind his saddle and helped tie the bear skin to the trader's mule.

"Headin' to Corydon Rose's place, on my way to Ourey," Buck said.

"That's where I'm going, too."

Buck nodded. "Well then, it looks like you've got yourself a travel companion."

So be it.

The men descended the incline and rode on until after sunset, when they decided to stop for the night. Yiska made a fire, and they cooked a supper of fresh bear meat and canned beans. As the temperature dropped, they retreated to the lean-to they'd put up.

Under pine bough shelter, Yiska reclined against his saddle with his Navajo blanket as his cover and new rifle at his side. The howl of coyotes echoed in the distance as he thanked the Christian God that He had heard his call for help today.

≈

Eliana, now dressed as the young man Eli, hummed as she sat on the bench next to Papa. He drove their wagon along the dirt toll road toward Eureka—one of several assignments they had contracted in photographing the mining towns throughout the San Juans. Their white mule, Sampson, pulled a box-covered wagon with Van Horn Photography painted on its sides. It housed a darkroom and temporary shelter for the pair.

"Did you hear Mr. Whiley at the hymn sing? He is quite a talented baritone," Eliana said.

"He carried quite a tune, I'll give him that. He actually knew some of those hymns," Papa said.

"He and Maria harmonized very well together." Eliana smiled at the thought of the unlikely couple.

Papa tugged on the reins and held his head high. "What I really enjoyed was the sound of my lovely daughter's voice."

Eliana smiled. "I do love to sing, and it was wonderful to hear all those people gathered together to worship. I'm glad we'll have a church in Lake City next year."

Papa gave a light snap of the whip. "Come on, Sampson, giddyup. At this rate, it will take us until next week to get to Eureka."

"Mr. Whiley seems quite smitten with Maria," Eliana said. "You never know, they might be the first couple to get married in that new church."

"Trask Whiley married. I've heard stranger things," Papa said.

At last they came to the hill that overlooked the mining town, and Papa pulled the wagon to a stop. Plats of stick houses and log cabins were set in rows near the Sunny Side Mine, built stair-stepped up the mountainside. "This is a good view," he said. "We'll set up here. Then we can go down into the town and get pictures there."

Eliana hopped down from the wagon, tucked her shirt into her trousers, adjusted her suspenders, and checked the buttons of her extra-large vest. She tucked some stray hairs back under her hat. Her shoulder-length hair was tied back with a piece of rawhide. No one could see her here, but it was better to be safe.

Eliana and Papa unloaded their equipment. They set up a stereo camera, which would use wet-glass plates to create stereographs. They'd decided, however, that when they were on the Robbins expedition they'd only use the dry process method. That way there would be no need to develop the pictures in the field, as they would bring the plates home for processing. Nor would they have to worry about glass breaking. Nevertheless, Papa still planned to bring a small, collapsible darkroom, since they would be leaving the wagon behind.

Eliana adjusted the lens of her camera and turned to Papa. "What made you change your mind about Yiska?"

"It troubled me when I learned he knew about your disguise," Papa said. "I thought his knowing would jeopardize your secret."

Eliana flattened her lips and listened.

"I've been able to get to know Yiska better since then, Sunshine. I would trust him with my life. . .and yours. In fact, it will probably be good that he does know—he may be able to help protect you." Papa brushed his hand over his beard. "But I *will* warn him to keep a proper distance from you."

Eliana sighed. She supposed Papa was right, but how she longed to spend time with Yiska. If only someone could get word to him in time about the opportunity to work with the Robbins survey. *Heavenly Father, in Your way, would You please see to it that Yiska will find out? You know, above all, what this will mean to him.*

&

Men gathered around Yiska and Buck as the trader displayed the bear fur outside Rose's Cabin. Buck hoped to impress the men enough for someone to make a trade. "It's a beauty, ain't it? I traded it with an Injun. Came upon him while he was dressing it and offered to help. Three brown bears had attacked him. Scared two of 'em off, but he shot this one dead, right before it plowed him off a cliff." Buck looked up at Yiska. "At least that's what Yiska tells me. He's the one who shot it!"

The men eyed Yiska up and down.

"What do you say? Can anyone offer me a fair trade or a nugget of gold?" Buck asked.

A man sidled up to Yiska. "Is that story true, young man?"

"More or less," Yiska said.

"Well then, it's a good thing I was praying for you. You nearly lost your life."

Hands in his pockets, Yiska leaned his weight back on one leg and narrowed his eyes. "Beg your pardon?"

"You heard right. Your name's Yiska, is that right? Yiska Wilcox?" the man asked. "I've been waiting for you. I have a message from Trask Whiley."

Yiska stared at him. "Do you need a guide?"

"No, but I could use a traveling companion on my way down to Silverton. My name's George Darley."

The men walked away from the group and stopped to talk under some trees. Yiska took off his hat and brushed the hair from his face. "What's this message from Whiley?"

"He wants you to go on the Chandler Robbins survey. He said you know the details."

Yiska broke into a grin. "Thank you. That's good news."

"There's more," Darley said.

Yiska cocked his head. "What's that?"

"Mr. Wilson from the *San Juan Prospector* wants to hire you to be a correspondent during the expedition. Mr. Whiley was in full support. Mr. Van Horn thought it was a good idea as well. They both were concerned that you get the good news in time, in case you missed Van Horn in Silverton." Darley smiled. "There was also a pretty young lady there who was hoping very much that I'd meet up with you."

Eliana. Yiska shook the man's hand. "Thank you, Mr. Darley."

"My pleasure." Darley smiled. "They gave me the message, and I've been praying for you ever since."

Yiska blinked. "Praying, you say. I've been doing a little of that myself."

"By the looks of that bear skin, I'd say you'd be crazy not to."

twelve

Yiska traveled with Mr. Darley southwest through the hilly countryside on horseback. How he ended up traveling with a preacher was beyond him. Yiska expected to hear sermons for miles on end, but Darley entertained him with tales of his journeys. He showed genuine interest in Yiska's travels as well. When Darley did mention God, it was in a natural way that didn't bother Yiska. Darley didn't scold the way Trask's father did back when Yiska worked at his trading post. Instead, Mr. Darley spoke of God as an old friend. Someone he respected and trusted. A traveling companion.

High in the hills, the two dismounted to stretch their legs and rest for a bit. They walked to the edge of a bluff and admired the way the mountains hugged the river below. Although some ice still encrusted its edge, the river flowed freely, and the flora hinted summer was on its way. Yiska took off his gloves and stuffed them in his coat pockets. "It's been a mild spring. The weather's on our side."

Mr. Darley loosened his scarf. "Do you remember that fierce snowstorm in May a few years back?"

"Sure do."

"I'll never forget it," Mr. Darley said. "I set out for Silverton across the old San Juan Trail after preaching at Hell's Acre. I went with Gus Talbot, the mail carrier, that day. No different than any other. When we got to Burrows Park, away from the timberline, we had to snowshoe it over the range, since the thaw was late. The clouds gathered, and if we quit walking, we were likely to freeze to death." Darley looked out over the mountaintops, shielding his eyes from the sun. "The snow came down hard. We could barely see to put one foot in front of the other. Both of us stepped right off a steep cliff, tumbled twenty feet down into the gulch. If the Lord didn't hear me call out to Him then, I would've supposed He was deaf."

"I'm beginning to think He does listen," Yiska said.

"I lived to tell about it, didn't I?" Mr. Darley grinned.

"I've asked for His help three times lately—when they threw me in jail for saving Miss Van Horn, when our stagecoach was attacked by renegade Utes, and during my run-in with the bears." Yiska remained quiet for a moment. "Why God would answer me, I don't know. Maybe others were praying and He heard them instead."

"That's an interesting thought. I've often wondered the same thing."

"You? But you're doing God's work."

"True. Though it's not the work we do that gets His attention. It's a humble heart that seeks Him." Darley folded his arms across his chest and looked Yiska in the eye. "He hears us because of His love for us, nothing more. Doesn't matter how loudly we call out to Him. Like when I shouted out during that blizzard. He heard me all right, but I have no doubt He was also attentive to the quiet prayers of a dear old lady who had it on her heart to pray for me during that storm."

"How'd she know you were in trouble?" Yiska asked.

"She saw me travel past her cabin on the old wagon road that day. Being the first woman in these parts, she knew the weather well and noticed how the clouds hung around the mountain peaks to the west. She grew concerned and prayed for my safety. A year later I saw her at a meeting, and she told me she'd never forget that terrible storm. I promptly agreed with her. She said she had it on her heart to pray for me until the storm let up, knowing I wouldn't relent until I reached my destination. I nearly wept when she told me."

Yiska thought about how he almost went on his own trek to Silverton, eager to conduct his interview after helping those miners up by Stony Pass. Had he done so, he would've missed the news about being hired as correspondent for the survey. And, by some miracle, he had survived the bear attack and made it up to Rose's Cabin, where Mr. Darley waited for him. Yet when Darley greeted him he said, *"I've been praying for you, young man."*

Yiska swallowed hard. He recalled the words Mrs. Whiley spoke to him when he left her home. *"God go with you. Remember that He is as close as a prayer."* He'd appreciated the kind words, but hadn't understood what they meant. Now he saw that the God they believed in was real. Perhaps this God even cared for him.

Yiska whisked a yellow jacket from his sleeve. A memory of Eliana the last night he had seen her came to his mind—of her in his buckskin coat. After taking it from her shoulders, he'd wrapped her in his arms and kissed her on the cheek. In turn she whispered in his ear, *"I'll keep you in my prayers, Yiska. Be well."* Her sentiment meant far more now.

The preacher continued. "I've learned it's one thing to call on God in urgent times, still another to trust Him daily on the path of life."

"Mr. Darley, you already *know* how to get to Silverton. Why'd you take me as a guide?"

Darley looked at Yiska as if amused. "Who's to say I'm not your guide for this part of the journey?"

Yiska smiled and shook his head. He looked out over the gorge and upward, holding the brim of his hat. He pointed to an eagle flying overhead.

"Magnificent creature," Darley said.

"They make it look so easy to soar on the wind like that."

"Perhaps it is, given the right conditions."

"Perhaps it is."

&

Eliana shifted her hips on the hard bench as the wagon jostled down the winding road toward Howardsville. The prosperous town hosted rows of storefronts and a multitude of cabins, unlike most of the other mining towns with merely a spattering of buildings. Papa had stopped whistling hours ago, a sign he was weary, too.

The white mule came to a complete stop. After an arduous trek over crude roads that wound their way around the Arastra Gulch mines, Sampson was exhausted.

Eliana exhaled, climbed down from the wagon, and took hold of his halter, urging him forward with a bit of sugar. "Just a little farther, boy." Once he resumed a sluggish pace, she hoisted herself back up beside Papa.

Although the late afternoon sun hid behind the clouds, she felt rather warm and unbuttoned her coat. Then she sneezed.

"Don't you catch a cold now, Sunshine," Papa said. "We don't need you pulling to a stop, too."

"It's the dust, Papa," she said. Or was it? *Lord, please don't let me get sick.*

Papa eyed her suspiciously. "We'll spend the night here and head down to Silverton the day after tomorrow."

"Day after tomorrow?" Eliana frowned. "We're so close. Shouldn't we be there already?" Sneezing again, she grabbed a handkerchief from her pocket.

"No need to worry. We've plenty of time yet, and Sampson isn't the only one that needs a rest."

"If we must." Eliana worried her lip.

"It's not like my Eli to pout," Papa teased. "I heard the hotel here pays special attention to women. It's unfortunate that they won't know you are one."

"Regardless, I intend to take a nice long bath and wash my hair—what little of it I have left." She reached back and adjusted the short ponytail behind her head. It had been nice to let it grow during the winter, but it was better this way for her disguise.

"Unlike you, seems like each winter that goes by I have less of my own to worry about." Papa chuckled.

"What do you mean? You still have a good head of hair." She lifted his hat from his head and set it back again and laughed.

Papa scratched his beard. "I think it's finding a new location on my chin. Speaking of which, did you bring some extra charcoal to darken your jaw?"

"Yes, Papa. I've thought of everything."

The following day, word got around that a photographer was in town, so Van Horn Photography set up shop in the hotel lobby. Papa spent the afternoon making tintypes for customers. Eliana remained upstairs in her room to nurse her cold—Papa's orders. Checking on her often, he brought her chicken soup and gingerroot tea. She passed the time reading her Bible, napping, and dreaming of Yiska.

She awoke the next morning with renewed energy. Her head began to clear. But raucous burros had brayed half the night, disturbing Papa's sleep. The songsters corralled next to the hotel hadn't bothered her at all. Papa had agreed to photograph the town buildings that morning, so Eliana offered to lend a hand.

"But you've hardly had time to recover." Papa yawned.

"I believe I'm more revived than you after that midnight serenade." Eliana ignored further protests and headed to the livery to fetch Sampson and the wagon.

After the productive morning, the mayor treated them to a wonderful meal of roast wild turkey and sweet potatoes at the Hungry Burro—though Papa didn't find the name of the restaurant amusing in the least.

That afternoon, the gradual descent into the valley of Silverton proved much easier on Sampson, and on the Van Horns. Eliana admired the snow-crowned mountaintops and the valley cloaked in green.

"The Silver Queen." She sighed. "How pleasant to meet you, your majesty." *Have you seen my handsome prince?*

Papa left the mule hitched outside the Earl Hotel while he and his "son" took their baggage inside. Eliana didn't mind playing the role but had to keep her awe in check when she saw the splendor of the beautiful hotel where they would spend the next few days.

When they went back outside, a crowd surged down the boardwalk. An old fellow plowed into Eliana. With nothing but a "Pardon me, lad," he continued on his way.

"What's all the commotion?" Papa asked a passerby.

"There's a preacher in town. Called a meeting at the Last Call Saloon."

"It must be Reverend Darley," Eliana said. Would he have news of Yiska?

"That's no place for a…for you." Papa caught his near miss when someone walked by. "Bring Sampson and the wagon over to the livery, Eli, and then you can go back to the hotel and relax. I'd like to hear Reverend Darley preach. And I'll find out if he got word to Yiska."

Disappointed, she untied Sampson, climbed aboard, and took the reins. "I'll see you back at the hotel."

After delivering the wagon and mule, she stepped outside the livery and shoved her hands into her pockets. She looked down the road at the mob entering one of the saloons. It wasn't fair that she couldn't go hear the reverend preach, but no reputable woman would dare set foot in a place called the Last Call Saloon. Then again, "Eli" Van Horn could go in her stead. She dusted the dirt from her sleeves and swaggered down the street.

With her shoulders held back, Eliana stepped into the saloon and made her way through the throng of men and unfamiliar odors. Every nook filled with eager men waiting to hear what the minister had to say, whether out of sincerity or curiosity. At the far end of the long room she saw Papa. She'd keep to the rear, well out of his view. She shuffled past men of all ages, some in day suits, but most in work clothes. A voluptuous woman in a knee-length, low-cut dress of red satin and black lace pushed past her. Eliana found a barrel in the corner and hopped up. Even so, she could only get an intermittent glimpse of Reverend Darley as the crowd shifted around her. But at least she could hear the message.

Dice scattered on the floor as Reverend Darley rallied an

audience by pounding his fist on a faro table. "Gentlemen, such a fine day to meet with you. I appreciate your taking a break from gambling to hear the Word of the good Lord."

As Darley surveyed his murmuring audience, Eliana scanned the sea of hats before her. She hoped to catch sight of a certain dented one, but she knew it was unlikely that Yiska would patronize a saloon, even if he was in town.

Darley extended his hand, revealing a silver piece. The crowd hushed. "I found this Spanish coin along the Old Spanish Trail. I thought I'd discovered silver when I saw it sparkle in the sunlight. It was silver all right, but I was fooled. What I found was evidence that men have searched for treasure in these parts for centuries." He lowered the volume of his voice, and all paid careful attention. "Folks have found coins and tools left by the Spaniards when they mined these very mountains. Many of those places remain hidden, because they were without the means to mine the lode in this dangerous place. Nor did they want to pay the king his royal fifth." A few in the assembly chuckled. "Indians buried the mines because they valued land more than mineral. Today we have but legends and hearty souls like you."

"Do you know where the treasure is, Brother Darley?" someone shouted.

"I reckon I do," he said, and all the men listened. "Silverton got its name because, although there isn't much gold here, you have silver by the ton." Men raised their glasses and cheered.

"Not so long ago, they called your fine town Baker's Park. Charles Baker's team came here looking for gold but missed the silver altogether."

"That's right, he did, leaving more for us," a voice mocked. Laughter erupted around the room.

"Job said, 'Surely there is a vein for the silver, and a place for the gold where they fine it.' A prospector once argued me on that passage saying the word 'fine' should be 'find.'

A prospector always hopes to find hidden treasure. But this verse refers to the found treasure that must be extracted and purified. Many of you know the treasure I'm speaking of. You've heard about it from your youth, but left it back east in pursuit of the San Juan bonanza. What have you forsaken to go after riches that remain hidden, when a greater treasure lies in God's Word?"

The men were silent. Eliana fought her fatigue, not wanting to miss a single word of the message.

"Friends!" Eliana jumped at the preacher's resounding voice. "While you are trying to strike it rich on earth, remember there is a greater lode in heaven."

Eliana sneezed and rubbed the tip of her nose with the back of her gloved hand. To her dismay, when she looked up her gaze fixed on a familiar set of eyes.

thirteen

Mutual recognition prompted Eliana to scoot through the side door and follow her acquaintance into the back alley. "Mr. Crawford, whatever are you doing here in Silverton?"

Cornelius Crawford eyed her up and down, perusing her male attire. "I could ask you the same thing"—he snickered—"*Miss* Van Horn."

Eliana's face heated. "Oh please, Mr. Crawford, promise me you will not give my identity away," she whispered. "It's a matter of safety."

"Promise? Like you promised to take my photograph back in Del Norte?" Cornelius chided.

"I do apologize, but I never saw you again, nor did you come see us."

"Suppose you have a point there. Tell me, little missy, what are you doing dressed like a feller? Ya almost had me fooled, 'cept for those pretty eyes of yours."

A deep voice penetrated the still air. "I'd like to know the answer to that myself." Eliana's eyes widened. It was Grover, one of those evil men who put Yiska in jail.

"Out of the way, old man. I have a little unfinished business with the lady." Grover pointed his revolver at Cornelius and slithered toward Eliana, hunger in his eyes. Cornelius scurried down the boardwalk away from the gun.

Eliana inched backward but found herself against a wall. Grover leaned in against her. Her stomach lurched, and she pushed uselessly against his chest.

❧

Thwack! Yiska's hatchet pinned Eliana's attacker to the building by the sleeve of his duster. She ducked out of the way as Yiska jumped the brute and thrust his gun into the man's back.

As he retrieved his hatchet, the man's coat ripped.

"Easy there, that's new," the brute growled.

Yiska grabbed him by the collar. "Put your hands on your head and turn around. Slowly."

Grover. One of the thugs from Del Norte. "Had a feelin' I'd see you again."

Cornelius Crawford reappeared with the law in tow.

"I'll be glad to take him off your hands."

Yiska looked around to find the deputy sheriff behind him, eyeing them suspiciously.

Eliana stepped forward. "Mr. Crawford. This man in the duster is the one who attacked me, is it not?"

"Yes, miss. . .mister," Crawford said.

Eliana smiled. The man had redeemed himself at last. She heaved a deep sigh and pulled her hat lower as the deputy hauled Grover away.

"Thank you, Mr. Crawford. You've done a good thing."

"I may be down on my own luck, but you can count on me."

Eliana opened her mouth as if to speak.

A chorus of "Amens" arose from inside the saloon. Yiska stepped between the pair and ushered them back inside the saloon. He squeezed Eliana's arm. "We've a sermon to finish hearing."

The crowd inside the Last Call seemed even more attentive than before. Reverend Darley did have a convincing way about him.

The preacher continued his discourse. "The wealth hidden in the earth cannot be obtained easily. Men must work to contrive ways to get the hidden treasure into their hands."

"He's got that right," Crawford whispered.

Yiska elbowed him and then caught Eliana's gaze. She immediately lowered her lashes. Despite her attire, she looked every bit as pleasing as he remembered. His heart raced.

"Consider the miners then. Let their courage, diligence, and constancy in seeking the wealth that perishes urge us to seek true riches. The great King Solomon said it is far better to get wisdom than silver or gold. Yet these minerals are sought and grace neglected. Should not the certain prospect of heavenly riches compel us more? Come, your heavenly Father beckons you, His gift of grace waiting to bestow."

Tears streamed down Crawford's cheeks. "Lord, have mercy on this sinner," he whispered.

A chorus of men began to sing a hymn, and others joined in. Yiska watched as Cornelius Crawford and several other contrite souls stepped forward and met Reverend Darley in front of the faro table. Yiska bowed his head in respect as Darley ended the meeting in prayer. When he looked up, Eliana was gone.

❧

Eliana hurried to the hotel and up the stairs to the Van Horns' suite. Once inside, she leaned against the closed door to catch her breath. She flung her hat onto the settee and scrubbed her face at the washstand. In the mirror, she studied her disheveled reflection. How could she make herself presentable? Surely Yiska would come to find her.

Eliana brushed her hair in haste and secured it in a celluloid headband, allowing her locks to hang onto her shoulders. In her private room, she pulled off her boots and rummaged for the one dress she had packed, a light brown gingham. Her lace-up boots were nowhere to be had. Slippers would have to do. She passed through the heavily draped doorway to the parlor, where she plucked a few petals from a fresh bouquet sitting on the center table. She crushed the petals in her palm and rubbed the scent against her wrists and the back of her neck, hoping she wouldn't smell like. . .a man.

No sooner had she plopped down on the settee and shoved her hat behind it, than a knock sounded at the door. She stood, smoothing her dress, and went to greet her company. She opened the door a crack. Piercing brown eyes stared back at her.

"Yiska, please come in. Papa will be here soon." She opened the door and beckoned him into the room as if nothing were out of the ordinary. "I was hoping to see you."

"Were you? Why did you leave the saloon?"

Eliana could feel the warmth creep up her neck. Hand to her chest she said, "You must be having a delusion. Or perhaps you have me confused with someone else."

His eyes narrowed beneath the brim of his hat. "They say everyone has a twin."

"Do they?" she asked nonchalantly. "Let me take your hat. Is this new?"

Yiska took it from his head and deposited it on hers. "Yup. That's about right." He rubbed his jaw with his thumb, indicating with the angle of his mouth that there must be a remnant of charcoal grease still on her face. Instant recollection of the first time they met, when she had newsprint all over her chin, made her face color again.

"Don't do that," Yiska said.

"What?" she asked.

"Blush."

"I'm sorry." Eliana's cheeks flamed even more.

He tossed the hat on a chair. "You know, you are irresistible. . . even dressed like a cowhand."

She swatted the air. "Cowhand?"

Yiska laughed.

"It's embarrassing to have you see me like that." Eliana winced in shame.

A slight curve appeared at corner of his mouth.

"Thank you for protecting me from Grover. I only wish he could have heard Reverend Darley's message. It might have had a positive impact on him."

Yiska shrugged. "Let's hope a little jail time will have a similar effect."

"I'm surprised that you were at the saloon," she said. "As I recall, you haven't a fondness for them."

"The preacher invited me. How could I say no?" Yiska's brow wrinkled. "He's a very convincing man."

"That he is." Eliana walked to the window and fingered

the lace curtain as she looked into the street. Hoping for some cool air, she attempted to open the window.

Yiska came up behind her. "Here, let me do that."

As the gentle breeze entered the room she turned to him. "How did you know I was there and in trouble?"

He hesitated. "I prayed for you. Then I heard a sneeze and when I turned around, I saw you in the back. I went to find you, but you'd disappeared. Figured you might have seen me and left out the back."

"I never saw you, though I did see Cornelius. I followed him to the alley to ask him to keep my identity secret. That's when Grover showed up." Eliana cocked her head and grinned. "Did you say you prayed for me?"

Yiska nodded. "I did."

A flood of reassurance washed over her.

"You'll have to get used to the fact that I'll see you in your disguise," Yiska said.

"You're going on the survey!" Eliana's mouth blossomed into a smile.

"I am. Mr.—I mean, Reverend Darley found me at Rose's Cabin and gave me the good news. I hoped I'd find you here and not have to wait until the rendezvous at Animas City."

"I'm glad you found me," Eliana said, her voice barely above a whisper.

Yiska stepped closer. "Like a hidden treasure." He lifted a hand and toyed with her hair. Then he brushed the back of his fingers over her cheek and lower lip with a featherlight touch.

Her stomach tightened and she tried to remain calm. Was he going to kiss her again?

᠀

"Look who I found in the restaur—" Papa burst through the doorway holding a tray of dishes with their evening meal. Reverend Darley, behind him, carried another.

Yiska stepped back from Eliana and rushed toward the door to assist Papa. "Mr. Van Horn. Reverend Darley. How good to see you. Let me take that." He took the tray and set it on the table then retrieved the other from the minister.

Eliana faced the window for a moment, hoping the fresh air would cool her cheeks. Then she turned to greet them. What must he and Papa have thought when they opened the door?

"It is a pleasure to see you again, Miss Van Horn," Reverend Darley said. "Though your father warned me I might find you in different attire. You look lovely."

"That you do, daughter." Papa kissed her on the cheek. He couldn't be too upset.

As she approached the table, the aroma of rosemary and thyme greeted her senses. Generous servings of beef, new potatoes, and a medley of vegetables filled four plates.

"There's enough for four. Are we expecting company?" Eliana asked Papa.

Papa look at Yiska. "I believe he is already here. You're welcome to join us, Yiska. In fact, this plate is for you. George told me you were in town, and I had a suspicion that we'd see you sooner rather than later."

Yiska looked at the mountain of food. "Much obliged. I can't recall the last time I saw such a feast."

"Let's sit then," Eliana said. "Reverend Darley, we'd be honored if you would ask the blessing on the meal."

Following the prayer they ate quietly, enjoying the food. After Papa took his last bite, he removed the cloth napkin tucked in his vest and wiped his mouth. "Yiska, we were concerned that you wouldn't get the word in time to go on the expedition. You must be thrilled to be going on the survey. And, by the way, we're right proud of you."

"Thank you, Mr. Van Horn."

Fearful her emotions would betray her, Eliana lowered her gaze. She retired to the settee and listened as the men continued the conversation.

"God has a way of making divine appointments," Darley said. "Isn't that right, Yiska?"

"It was good timing meeting up with Reverend Darley. He's been entertaining me with his tall tales all the way down from Rose's Cabin," Yiska said.

Darley placed his hand on Yiska's shoulder. "This young man has a tale of his own to tell. Something about a little meeting with a family of bears."

Yiska recounted his adventure in his humble way. "It means a lot to know that folks were praying for me. Guess that's what spared my life." When his gaze met Eliana's, his eyes glowed with appreciation for her prayers. A quiet understanding grew between them, and a restful peace came over Eliana, inducing her sleepy eyes to close.

"Papa." Eliana awoke as her father covered her with an afghan. She lay reclined on the settee, the room dark except for the faint light of a gasolier. Both Reverend Darley and Yiska had left. When had she dozed off?

"You might want to get up and sleep in your bed. It might be your last time sleeping in comfort for a while. I'm going to turn in now, too. Good night, Sunshine." He kissed her on the cheek.

"I will. Good night, Papa."

He walked toward the bedchambers then stopped and turned back. "God bless you."

"What's that for?" she asked.

"When you sneezed during Reverend Darley's sermon today."

fourteen

Yiska, Eliana, and Papa set out at dawn on horses obtained from the Silverton Livery with Sampson in tow, packed to the hilt with provisions and photography equipment. Yiska and Papa had mailed the interview and photograph of Mr. Snowden to the *San Juan Prospector*. Yiska also notified Mr. Wilson that he was pleased to accept his new assignment as a correspondent for the Robbins survey and asked him to inform Mr. Whiley. Now they were on their way to rendezvous with Chandler Robbins.

Hymns of praise flowed from Eliana's joyful heart. Refraining from singing at the top of her lungs, she sang softly, "Fairest Lord Jesus, ruler of all nature..."

Yiska's smile flashed in the sunlight as he pulled up beside her on Shadow. "Don't stop on account of me."

Papa rode up beside them. "I'm afraid she's not one to sing for an audience, though my songbird is worthy of one."

Eliana hoped that the shade from her hat would shelter her face from the bright sun that so easily tanned her complexion, as well as hide the blush that warmed her cheeks.

Yiska pointed from the narrow canyon to the tempestuous Animas River raging between the Needle Mountains. "This river is a terrible serpent. Not even passable at some points. We follow it all the way to Animas City. Don't ride too close to the edge. It's too rocky, and there's not enough shade. Keep to the tree line, and it will give us some protection and make the ride smoother."

The river reflected the azure sky on the almost cloudless day. The temperature warmed as they headed farther south. Eliana removed her overcoat and tied it behind her saddle. By noon the small convoy found an embankment by the river under the shade of the tall pines. She was glad for the respite from the struggle she'd had all morning with her ornery mount, Firefly.

After they'd eaten a frugal lunch, Papa put his pipe back in his pocket and checked Sampson's line. "Time to move on, Eliana." He mounted and rode back up the rocky incline.

"C'mon Firefly, you've had your nourishment." Eliana coaxed her willful horse with a firm tug and braced her boots on the stony ground by the river's edge, trying not to slip. She whistled and clucked as she pulled the horse's reins. "Firefly. Git. Git up here!"

Yiska rode out of the shade. "Stubborn," he said.

"That mare or my daughter?" Papa asked.

Eliana turned and looked at the two men. Yiska's grin didn't escape her notice as he rode by on Shadow. "I could use a little assistance here, gentlemen." She yanked on Firefly's halter, but the mare wouldn't budge.

"You're doing fine, dear. She won't obey you unless you learn to handle her yourself."

"Fine." She begged, she pleaded, and to her own chagrin, she nearly cussed. Her face flushed. She glared at the men, daring them to say a word.

Yiska called out over his shoulder, "You'll catch more flies with honey than with vinegar."

"Some old Indian saying?" Her father chortled.

Yiska hiked his chin and grinned. "Something Mrs. Whiley used to say."

"Well, if there were any honey in this forsaken place, I'd give her some," Eliana huffed.

Yiska made some high pitched kissing sounds. Firefly immediately raised her head, dug in her hooves, and came up the embankment—Eliana in tow. Yiska issued a satisfied nod.

"How'd you do that?" she asked.

"Like this." He pursed his lips together once again.

Eliana glared at him and shot a glance at her father, relieved that he was looking away. "Yiska. . ." she whispered, between clenched teeth. "How did you know it would *work*?" She cocked her head. "Some secret way of the Navajo?"

"Let's see. You made every other sound possible. Figured I'd give that one a try."

"Well, thank you. I've more experience with mules than with horses."

"My pleasure." Yiska patted Shadow on the neck and put light pressure on the animal's belly with one knee. The horse turned and proceeded toward the ridge. He trotted ahead to scout out the trail.

"Show off," she muttered under her breath.

Papa let out a chuckle at the exchange and pulled his own horse around. "He's all right in my book. But you'd best mind your manners."

"My manners?" Eliana asked.

"Don't want to stir up any trouble, especially after we get to the rendezvous."

"Would you care to explain?"

Papa pinched his eyebrows to let her know he was serious. "We have a lot of miles yet to travel. Don't encourage him."

Eliana tried to ignore the accusation and let out an exasperated breath. With one foot in the stirrup, she hoisted herself up on Firefly. Papa didn't really think she'd risk the expedition by entertaining notions of romance, did he? With a kissing noise she urged her horse forward.

❧

After a rough twenty-four miles from Silverton, Yiska led the Van Horns to the shelter of ponderosa pines to camp for the night. He dismounted and took in a deep breath of the pine scented air then gathered branches and leaves to prepare a lean-to while Eliana and Mr. Van Horn set up their small canvas tents. They gave the horses and mule some oats and water from the stream. Then Yiska stretched a line between two trees and tethered the animals. He made a fire, and Mr. Van Horn heated some canned hash, boiled some coffee, and offered a prayer of thanks. After they ate, Van Horn read a short passage out loud from his Bible. As they sat around the campfire in the twilight of the early June evening, they listened to the sounds of the rushing river and chirping tree frogs.

"We made good progress today. You both did well when we had to ride up those ridges. The rest of the way will go a little easier." Yiska stirred the fire with the end of a branch. "We should get to Baker's Bridge by late morning."

"How far is that?" Eliana asked.

"About ten or twelve miles," he said. "Then another twelve to Animas City. We should get there by sundown tomorrow."

Eliana let out a deep sigh. "I'll be so glad to get there." She rubbed her legs. "I'm so tired and sore."

Mr. Van Horn tapped his empty pipe on his knee. "You're not used to all the riding. But I'm afraid there'll be much more of it ahead, my dear. The expedition hasn't even commenced." He raised an eyebrow. "Other than that, how are you holding up? I haven't heard any sneezing."

Eliana stretched, issuing a low moan when her body protested. She mumbled as she lumbered toward the river's edge. "I'm fine.... It's the other end I'm worried about."

Yiska cocked his head, covering his mouth to smother a laugh.

Van Horn chuckled as he got up, Bible in hand. "I'll turn in now so I can be up for the second watch."

Eliana placed her fingertips on her lips then turned them toward her father, sending him a good-night kiss. "Sleep well, Papa. I'll go to my tent shortly."

Yiska observed the closeness between the two. They meant everything to each other.

"Be sure to wake me, Yiska," Van Horn said.

"You bet." Although they weren't in hostile Indian territory, small parties kept guard. There was always the danger of wild animals or the occasional desperate soul who ran dry while prospecting the river to beware of. Good thing Eliana could handle a weapon.

Yiska wandered to where she stood, her silhouette like a male. But underneath the manly clothes, he knew she was every bit a woman—the woman he was falling hard for.

Eliana took off her hat and untied the cord from her hair, her tousled locks falling around her face. Her hat dropped to the ground, and Yiska picked it up. Their eyes met as he handed it to her, but neither of them spoke.

The firelight, reflected in her eyes and gave the illusion that he could see deep into her heart. He longed to kiss her, passionately, as he did the first time their lips met, but he dared not. He had to train himself to keep a proper emotional distance for the expedition. Maybe when it was over. . .

A branch snapped. Eliana let out a tiny gasp. Their heads darted in the direction of the noise, Yiska's hand ready at his side. He caught a glimpse of the white tails of deer fleeing into the woods.

Eliana sighed in relief. "Perhaps I'm not cut out for this." She turned and took a few steps away.

Yiska walked up behind her and wrapped his arms around her. With his head nestled over her shoulder he spoke into her ear in a low voice. "Eliana, this is your dream. Every moment, all of it. Even when you're tired or afraid. You're braver than you realize, and you will do this, and do it well."

She sniffed and put her hand up to her face to wipe her tears. She clung to his arms, and her breathing relaxed. There they stayed as one, watching the light of the moon dance upon the river.

&

When Eliana awoke the next morning before dawn, breakfast was already cooking on the fire, and Cornelius Crawford was serving it up.

"Mornin' Miss. . .I mean, young man." His whiskered cheeks framed a toothless grin. "I came in last night after you all had retired. I'd have caught up with you sooner, but I got a little off track. Betcha didn't know I'm going on that survey expedition to New Mexico with you."

Astonished, Eliana placed both hands on her hips. "I'm surprised you're leaving your mine behind."

Papa and Yiska emerged from their shelters dumbfounded.

"You didn't say anything about that when you came into camp last night," Yiska said.

Cornelius handed Eliana a plate of beans, bacon, and biscuits. "Told you I was down on my luck. Lost my gold claim in a card game. But since I gave my heart to Jesus, He's been blessin' me and helping me get my life in order. I gave up the whiskey and even got me a job."

"I take it you have a job on the expedition then," Papa said.

"Sure do. I wuz hired as the cook. Providin' I can get down to Animas City in time." Cornelius chewed on a piece of bacon and smacked his lips.

"All this in a matter of a couple of days, Crawford?" Yiska asked.

"You betcha," the reformed miner said.

Papa chuckled. "Sounds like a genuine miracle. Glad to have you along." Yiska choked on his coffee and shook his head.

They rode along at a good pace, making their way through the gorge. Eliana breathed in the fresh morning air and relaxed as she and Firefly fell into a steady gait. Peacefulness permeated her heart as she remembered Yiska's soothing words the night before, and the thought of his masculine arms around her.

Yiska rode ahead to scout then circled around to meet the group. "Baker's Bridge is up ahead."

"That's the bridge Charles Baker and his team built back in the sixties, during the gold boom," Papa said. "I'd like to photograph it if you think we can afford the time."

"We'll cross and rest for a spell. Then you can get your pictures," Yiska said.

Eliana contemplated the narrow section of the river where logs were strewn together from one thick section of rock to another. "Is it safe?"

"It's as safe as it ever was." Without hesitation Yiska rode Shadow across and waited on the other side. Papa followed, Sampson trailing behind him. Cornelius came along next on a coal-colored mule loaded with pots and pans.

Eliana sat on Firefly and urged her to cross the bridge, but the horse seemed frightened of the water rushing underneath. Firefly's hooves clopped up and down on the logs, and then she backed up. Eliana tried to ease her forward once again then increased pressure with her heels.

The horse reared and threw Eliana to the ground with a thud. The force pushed the wind from her lungs and left her gasping for breath.

fifteen

Eliana coughed and struggled to resume breathing while Yiska and Papa raced across the bridge. They crouched beside her side as she lay on the hard ground.

Beads of perspiration dotted Papa's brow over eyes filled with alarm. "Sunshine, are you all right?"

Eliana clamped her teeth together and grimaced in pain as she attempted to get up.

"Stay still for a minute," Papa said. "You're awfully pale."

"I'm fine, Papa. Please help me sit." The croak in her voice did little to convince even her.

"How can you be fine? That crazy animal just threw you."

When he hesitated, she grabbed his arm and yanked herself to a sitting position. Pain exploded through her body like dynamite in a cave. She took a shaky breath, opened and closed her hands, and made circles with her wrists. Her body seemed to be in working order. Nothing broken. Deep, pebble-filled scratches crisscrossed her palms. Why hadn't she left her gloves on?

Papa carefully brushed the grit from her hands. He then examined her head, feeling for bumps. "Is that tender? There's a small knot back there."

"It is rather sore, but not too bad," she said.

He patted her legs through her trousers, from her thighs all the way down to her boots. "Can you feel your legs?"

"Yes, Papa. Really, I'm fine." She hadn't seen him this worried about her since she fell out of the old oak tree when she was eleven years old. She'd climbed up to check the view of the pastures and fluffy clouds. If she could have figured out how to carry a camera up with her, she might have been able to take a picture of the nest of baby birds she discovered there.

As her thoughts floated about, she hadn't realized she was leaning back with her head against Yiska until she felt the rumble of his voice through his chest. "Should we move her?"

"Yes. Let's take her over there and make her comfortable," Papa said. *Oh, but Papa, I am comfortable here with Yiska.*

A slight groan escaped her when Papa scooped her up. Eliana felt limp as he cradled her in his arms then set her on a grassy hill and propped her against a fallen tree.

Papa bunched his coat behind her for comfort. She looked around to get her bearings.

Cornelius approached and handed Eliana a canteen of water. "Have some of this."

"Thank you. That's very kind of you."

"Yer welcome. Glad to see yer in one piece." The spry old man went back over the bridge, where he'd left the horses and pack animals tethered to an old fence post.

A shock of alarm ran through Eliana. "Firefly! Where. . . ?"

Papa placed his hand on her arm. "Yiska went after her."

She let out a sigh of relief. "Oh, good. He'll find her."

Minutes later Yiska appeared riding her mount, in full control. *My, he looks good on a horse.* Eliana chastised herself for taking such liberties with her thoughts—that fall must've made her giddy.

She widened her eyes as she addressed Yiska. "You're brave."

"She needs to know she can still be ridden." He leaned down and gently rubbed the mare's neck.

"I know. I'll ride her, if you can please get her across the bridge for me."

"That's what I intend to do. But can you ride? Are you hurt?"

His concern moved her. "I'm just sore. I've come this far, and nothing will stop me from going on that expedition." She remembered Yiska's encouraging words from last night and willed her gaze to show her determination.

Papa handed Eliana her hat, interrupting her thoughts.

"Eli Van Horn has spoken."

But the warmth in Yiska's eyes reflected hers, answering her unspoken message. "If you can make it another mile we'll noon somewhere special."

❧

Eliana rode Shadow for the next mile, while Yiska remained on Firefly. They came into an area with mists rising up from the ground. A huge mound of mineral-laden lava rock came into view. Steaming hot water flowed from the colorful lump into streams all around it.

Her eyes flashed at Yiska in delight. "Hot springs. The streams flow into heated pools of water. The Utes and Navajo have often fought over healing waters like this. I thought a soak might ease your pain—there's enough brush to give you privacy." His thoughtfulness sent a ripple of warmth through her. If the healing balm could be applied to her aching body she'd be whole. This man was taking hold of her entire being.

"Eliana."

She turned to face him.

"I'll show you where you can soak while Crawford fixes something to eat and I tend to the animals. Your Pa's unpacking his camera."

"Oh, that reminds me. He never did photograph Baker's Bridge."

Papa came up beside her. "That's all right, dear. Seeing you fall like that embedded a permanent image of the location in my mind. Reminds me of the time you fell from the oak tree when you were a child and broke your elbow."

Yiska's eyebrows lifted in amusement.

Eliana retreated to the spring. With the men at a discreet distance, she wrestled herself free from the binding around her chest and took the liberty of removing all but her undergarments. She descended into the therapeutic pool, welcoming the warmth and appreciating Yiska's thoughtfulness. She exhaled as she submerged and allowed the tension to dissipate, the hot mineral water soothing her aches and pains.

Through a small place in the vegetation she spied Yiska sitting on a boulder facing the opposite direction, writing in his journal. Papa approached, and they engaged in conversation. Then Yiska jumped up and stomped his boot. Papa rocked up and down on his toes. What were they arguing about?

ða.

Mr. Van Horn had never spoken to Yiska like that before. It took all the self-control he had to keep from raising his voice at the man, but he didn't want Eliana to hear them. The sparks that flew during that discussion could have ignited a stick of dynamite.

He knew her father worried about her. The stress of the day must have hit him, but Yiska had done nothing to deserve the condescending lecture. The man nearly blamed him for Eliana's accident. Mr. Van Horn demanded that Yiska do three things: keep her secret, keep her safe, and keep his distance. He understood Van Horn's implied warning—no romance. But when Yiska reminded him that he already had been seeing to her welfare, Van Horn reversed his tone. "If anything ever happens to me," he said, "I'm counting on you to continue to watch out for her."

The man didn't even have to ask.

At the lower elevation, the four travelers marveled as the range opened up into a beautiful valley dotted with several old log homes. Only a handful of families had lived there since the Baker party wintered there in '61, but more folks were moving in to reestablish Animas City. It thrilled Yiska to see Eliana's excitement. Her father's temperament returned to normal as if they'd never had that discussion.

The sun set as the small caravan rode over the grassy knoll, seeking out the trading post where they would find Chandler Robbins. Finally. They had arrived at the rendezvous.

ða.

Eliana climbed down from Shadow's back, a bit stiffly, while the others dismounted. Yiska grabbed Shadow's reins and handed the horses off to a hostler. They headed toward the trading post, where a man sat sketching the sunset. As he saw them approach, the man rose with a chuckle and made his way toward them.

Papa quickened his step and held out his hand. "Harland Mattheson? What in God's green earth are you doing in Animas City?"

Eliana recognized the name. Mr. Mattheson's thick beard, though whiter now, and his limp were also familiar. Although anxious to greet him, she hung back and kept her head low.

Reverend Mattheson slapped Papa on the back. "John, old friend. Chandler told me you'd be going on the survey as the official photographer. That was what finally convinced me to come along. Imagine. Three of us from the Ohio 86th Infantry back together again."

"It's great to see you, Harland. What has it been, seven or eight years?" Papa took Reverend Mattheson to the side and spoke to him in a low voice.

Reverend Mattheson looked at Eliana and grinned, and Papa beckoned her to come near. "Look at you. All grown up." Their longtime friend looked her up and down. "I must say you do look quite different from the last time I saw you"—he leaned closer and whispered—"as a girl." The man cleared his throat. "Don't worry; your secret is safe with me."

"Thank you, Reverend Mattheson. It's good to see you. We've missed you a great deal."

"I go by Mr. Mattheson these days. I haven't had a church for some time now. I've been keeping myself occupied as a naturalist."

"Yiska. Cornelius." Papa called the men over. "Harland Mattheson, this is Yiska Wilcox, correspondent for the *San Juan Prospector*. He's also our guide. And Cornelius Crawford, one of the best cooks around."

Eliana was proud of the way Papa made the introductions—especially the way he made Yiska sound so important.

Mr. Mattheson issued a nod. "Gentlemen. Pleased to make your acquaintance."

"Let's go inside and see Robbins and get you all something to eat. Though I'm sure it won't be nearly as good as Mr. Crawford's cooking, the owner's wife is serving up a nice stew and fresh bread."

Eliana was glad to see the old friend who baptized her as a girl. One thing she knew for sure—she could trust him to keep her identity confidential. He had at least one secret of his own.

⁊⁊

Inside the trading post, Papa saluted Chandler Robbins. "Sergeant."

"Lieutenant." Mr. Robbins returned the salute and shook Papa's hand. "John, it's good to see you after all these years. I'm glad Ryder recommended you when he couldn't get away."

"I appreciate that he did. He gave me my start. Taught me photography right on the battlefield." Eliana listened with interest, as her father seldom discussed his past.

"What about you?" Mr. Robbins asked. "I understand you do contract work for the GLO. They were pleased to have you sign on for the survey."

"I'm doing fairly well. It's hard work documenting the mining areas, but we also have a small studio up in Lake City to serve the community."

Mr. Robbins arched his thick eyebrows. "Hell's Acre?"

"That den of evil is only a remote section of town. The folks in Lake City officially established a fine town last year. There's even talk of building a church."

"Is that so?" Mr. Mattheson asked.

"Yes, George Darley was out recently. In fact, we heard him preach at home and then up in Silverton. He drew quite a crowd at the Last Call Saloon," Papa said.

Mr. Mattheson chortled. "Leave it to George. Can't say that I've heard a sermon in some time. But I've no one to blame for that but myself."

"John, you keep referring to 'we,'" Mr. Robbins said.

"Of course, excuse me." Papa called Eliana over, though she stood only a few feet away.

"This is Eli, my son and my photography assistant. This is Chandler Robbins."

With a nod, Eliana acknowledged the impressive, rugged man. She hoped he wouldn't think her rude for not shaking his hand, but hers still stung from the fall. Besides, she felt it would be proper if he made the advance first, since he was the man in charge.

"Sir, it's a pleasure to meet you. I've heard a great deal about you," she said in a masculine timbre.

Mr. Robbins dipped his chin. "If you're any bit like your father, I'm sure you'll be a great asset to the team."

Mr. Robbins regarded Papa. "Any other children?"

"No, only the one."

"And your wife?"

"I lost her several years ago."

"Must not have been easy raising a kid on your own, but I see he turned out all right." Mr. Robbins turned toward Eli.

Eliana shoved her hands in her pockets, her eyes scanning the gentlemen. Mr. Mattheson looked every bit as uncomfortable as her father. Papa cleared his throat and nodded.

"Watch yourself there!" Heads turned to see a disgruntled man of about thirty, who had been lingering nearby, wipe spilled coffee from the front of his suit.

"Pardon me." Yiska took a bandanna from his pocket and dabbed at the man's chest.

"Don't touch me! Who let this savage in here?" the well-dressed man barked.

Robbins walked up to the pair, and Papa followed. "Hold on now. It's just a little accident," Mr. Robbins said.

"Do you know how much I paid for this suit?"

"I don't want to know. You should have left it in New York City and brought proper clothing." Mr. Robbins made a point of scanning the worn and dusty outfits of the men around him. "Gentlemen, meet Warren Cates from *Atlantic Monthly Magazine*."

Warren Cates straightened as Mr. Robbins made the introductions. Then Robbins eyed Yiska. "I don't believe we've met."

Yiska's eyes shifted to Eliana's father and then back to Mr. Robbins again.

Papa interjected, "This is Yiska Wilcox. He's here to do feature work for the *San Juan Prospector*."

Mr. Robbins looked Yiska square in the face, as if he expected more. Papa continued, "Yiska is also your guide."

Robbins looked Yiska over with a satisfying nod then looked hard at the agitator. "Now hear that, Cates. Next to me, Mr. Wilcox is the most important person on this expedition, and I expect you to treat him as such."

Eliana doubted Robbins normally treated his guides with much respect, but he surely knew how to put Warren Cates in his place.

"I've heard you're one of the best guides around," Robbins said. "I wouldn't be surprised if your travels have given you plenty of interesting things to write about."

Mr. Cates harrumphed.

Eliana restrained herself from boasting about the Anonymous Explorer.

"Thank you. I've read some of your work and studied your maps. Superior detail," Yiska said.

"I appreciate your good opinion. More will be published next year—including this survey of the four corners." Robbins scratched behind his ear. "I'd like to go over the maps with you after you grab some supper, and then we'll all meet outdoors to go over the itinerary."

An hour later the entire survey team gathered around a campfire, fifteen in all.

"My goal is to confirm the coordinates from the Washington meridian and reset the marker at the intersection of Colorado, Utah, Arizona, and New Mexico," Robbins told them. "From there we'll go south to establish the boundary between the New Mexico and Arizona territories."

Eliana listened attentively to every word.

"I emphasize my goal. I've been commissioned by the U. S. General Land Office. All others have been hired on to support the mission. Some of you are joining us of your own volition, like Harland Mattheson, a naturalist, or on assignment, like the journalists Warren Cates and Yiska Wilcox."

Mr. Cates rolled his eyes.

"No one is indispensible, and I'll not hesitate to dismiss anyone who interferes with my progress."

Mr. Robbins looked at Yiska. "Wilcox will also serve as our guide. He has a few words about our journey."

Eliana felt so proud of Yiska, it was hard not to smile at him as he spoke. "We have over three hundred miles in all to travel, and although you can feel the chill in the air tonight, we will leave these mountains for the heat of the desert. We'll follow the Animas River south to New Mexico, where it joins the Rio San Juan. Don't underestimate the rivers. The Spaniards called the Animas the 'River of Lost Souls.'"

Yiska hadn't mentioned that before, and it struck Eliana as both eerie and poetic.

He continued. "But that isn't the only danger we might encounter. It's twenty miles to the border, and most of it is in Ute territory. Stay armed and together. If all goes well, we'll make it into New Mexico by nightfall tomorrow."

Robbins clapped his hands together. "All right, fellas, let's get to bed. We're pulling out at first light."

As the men adjourned, Eliana followed Yiska to tell him she thought he did a fine job explaining things.

Warren Cates got there first. " 'River of Lost Souls?' I heard the river got its name because that's where the Indians buried their enemy's bodies." Cates sneered at Yiska. "Don't go getting any ideas."

"Don't give him a reason," Eliana hissed.

Cates pivoted around. "Indian lover."

She'd defended Yiska again. Now what could she say? "He can take care of himself. But I don't like you carrying a grudge before we even begin the excursion. It's not fair to the team."

Cates started to grab her by the neck, but Yiska's arm flew up to stop him.

"Leave the kid alone and get out of here." The muscles in Yiska's jaw tightened.

Cates contorted his face and tromped off like an irritated mountain goat.

Yiska walked into the darkness without turning back. Eliana did not follow.

&

At daybreak Eliana and Papa took some photographs of the train of pack mules, wagons loaded with provisions, and armed men on horseback ready to embark on their journey. Chandler Robbins rode at the head of the column with Yiska beside him. She would not get to speak to Yiska to offer an apology until they stopped for a rest, but from what he explained about the Utes, she wasn't even sure that would happen. Eliana yawned as she put the camera back into the pack. She'd tossed and turned all night. She anticipated having trouble sleeping the night before the survey commenced, but all she thought about was the trouble she had made for Yiska. The pressure in her heart squeezed the joy right out of her.

Along the way, Papa and Mr. Mattheson enjoyed catching up on the years. Mr. Mattheson told Papa how he had become a naturalist. Some of his sketches and descriptions had even been published in a scientific journal. The sun rose high in the sky, and at last the convoy stopped to have a meal and rest the animals.

Papa and Mr. Mattheson sat on a log with their rifles propped by their sides, engrossed in conversation while eating their fill of fritters and coffee. Eliana went over to tend Firefly. She petted her nose and wondered if her mount was as sore as she was. Her body still complained from the harsh fall and longed for another soak in the hot springs.

Yiska appeared with Shadow in tow.

"You startled me," Eliana said.

He rested his hand on her saddle. "Have you watered her yet?"

"No. But I need to."

"Come with me."

They led their horses past Papa, Mr. Mattheson, and Mr. Robbins. "I'm taking Eli down to water his horse," Yiska called out.

Papa waved, hardly aware of their presence.

They traveled in silence to a small hill overlooking a wide stream. Aspens offered a shady retreat. Eliana found her confidence and faced Yiska. "I'm sorry. I shouldn't have defended you to Mr. Cates like that."

"You're right. You shouldn't have." She couldn't read anything into his flat tone. Was he angry? Of course he was.

Her eyes stung, but she refused to cry in front of him. "I'm going to take Firefly down to the stream."

"I'll go with you."

She looked back at him. "No. I mean, I need some privacy. I have a few things to tend to. Please keep your back turned."

Yiska's mouth drew into a tight line. "All right. Don't be long."

She led Firefly down the slope and let her drink from the clear mountain water. Eliana knelt down by her, cupped her hands, and took an icy sip. She tossed her hat to the ground, released her straggly plait, and shook out her hair. She would fix it in a moment. She spotted some high bushes nearby and retreated behind them to relieve herself. Now untucked, dare she adjust the bindings that camouflaged her figure?

She removed her neckerchief and unbuttoned down to the top of her underbodice. She knelt back down near the stream and splashed her face and neck, letting the water trickle down her chest. The days were growing hotter, as Yiska had warned. The frigid water and the gentle breeze invigorated her. In a few more hours they would reach New

Mexico, where they'd stop for the night. She could do this. It wasn't an easy journey, but she was determined to endure any hardship—including Yiska's disappointment in her, and her disappointment with herself. *Please Lord, let him forgive and trust me again.*

A hard lump caught in her throat as she tried not to weep. Pain intensified throughout her body. She lowered her head and released tears like a torrent.

A shadow flickered across her reflection in the water. She was not alone. Had Yiska come to find her?

A wave of fear assailed her. Eliana turned and gasped—a lone Ute Indian loomed in front of her.

Eliana struggled to get to her feet, but he lunged forward and held her with the sharp point of a knife to her neck. She stared into his black eyes and let out shallow breaths. Where was her voice now?

sixteen

Yiska pulled his journal from his saddlebag and fumbled through the pages. A page had been torn out, and Eliana's photograph was missing. The private words that he'd penned about Eliana up in the flowery basin—gone. Someone was up to no good.

Warren Cates. *He knows that Eli is a girl.* Yiska's chest tightened. Blood pulsed through the veins of his forearms as he squeezed the leather tome.

In the distance, Firefly neighed and stomped. Alarm ripped through his body. *Eliana!*

Yiska tore down the hill, boots stirring up dust and stones. Firefly pawed the ground, her nose pointing to the overgrowth. Adrenaline exploded through Yiska's body. He broke through the bushes and found Eliana pininoed against a boulder.

Yiska's breath seethed through clenched teeth as he flung himself onto her attacker. The Ute rolled over and sprang to his feet. Yiska lunged at him, grabbing his wrist so hard the bone dagger dropped from his grip. The Ute seized Yiska's waist and threw him to the ground. They wrestled over dirt and pine needles. Rocks cut into Yiska's shins.

Yiska straddled the warrior, pinning the man's body between his legs, and held his own knife at the enemy's neck. Piercing eyes of hot coal glared at him. *God, help me!*

A strange shift from anger to answer brought Yiska to his senses. To kill the man would bring more trouble. As he kept the Indian pinned to the ground, knife at his throat, Yiska spoke the Piute word for 'trade,' one of the survival words he knew. "*Nararwop.*"

His face like stone, the warrior issued a slight nod, acknowledging agreement.

Yiska sliced through the Indian's beaded bone neckpiece. A warning. He jerked his chin, motioning the man to get up.

The Ute stood resolute. The lean and muscular build above his breechcloth and leggings revealed brute strength. Yiska drew his revolver for insurance.

The Indian made a guttural sound as he angled his head toward Eliana, where she hovered on the ground. "*Mamachi.*"

With a sharp jab to his chest Yiska answered. "Mamachi— *My* woman."

Yiska pointed at Eliana's horse. "*Poonggo.*" He inched back and untied Firefly from the large root where Eliana had secured her. He had to appease the oppressor to ensure their safety.

The Indian took a step forward.

Yiska raised his hand, and the Ute halted. Yiska grabbed Eliana's rifle from the scabbard attached to her saddle and placed it on the ground behind him. He released Firefly's girth and tossed the saddle to the ground in one sweep— blanket, pack, and all. Yiska motioned for the Indian to come forward and stepped away from the horse.

The renegade whisked himself up on the mare's bare back and rode away with the force of a sandstorm, echoes of screams trailing behind him.

Yiska released the wind from his lungs and turned to Eliana. He pulled her to her feet and wrapped his arm around her waist as they ascended the steep incline, keeping his ear tuned to potential danger. He took Eliana's saddle and gear, hoisted it up in front of Shadow's saddle, and mounted his horse in one swift motion. Then he stretched his arm to Eliana and helped her up behind him.

She wrapped her arms around his waist and laid her head against his back. Yiska dug his heels into the sides of his faithful mount, and Shadow bolted. After riding a short distance, they stopped in a grove of piñon trees.

Yiska dismounted, placed a firm grip around Eliana's waist, and lowered her from his horse into his embrace.

"Will he return?" she asked.

"No. I'm sure of it. And if there were others, we'd have seen them by now." He stepped back and cupped her face in his hands. The very hands that had almost killed a man now held the one he loved. The mystery of it confounded him.

Eliana's eyes still held fear. "Why didn't you kill him?"

His eyes widened. "Is that what you wanted?"

Arms wrapped around him, she grabbed a fistful of his buckskin shirt in her hands. "No. But a few times I thought it might happen."

"If I killed him, there'd be more trouble to contend with. The Utes take a life for a life. None of us would be safe until they avenged him."

The fear in Eliana's eyes waned and became like dew.

Yiska swallowed hard. "I had to say that."

"That I am your woman?" Hazel eyes looked up at him from beneath her dark lashes.

"Yes."

She wet her lower lip. "Am I?"

Yiska leaned his forehead against hers, and they took in the same air with shallow breaths. As he brushed the hair from her face, he felt her tremble. She was shivering.

Yiska lowered his gaze and noticed a graceful neck and collarbone, soft enough to touch. Her top few buttons were undone. With gentle ministrations he fastened them, one by one. He could almost feel her beating heart, and knew she must feel the pounding of his when she placed her palm against his chest.

The thunder of hoofbeats came upon them, and a small posse of men pointed their rifles straight at Yiska.

❧

"Papa, no!" Eliana cried. Half a dozen men approached on horseback, looking more like a lynch mob than the cavalry.

Papa cocked his rifle. "That's my daughter you've got there. Move away from her."

"That's right, Wilcox. Nice and slow," Mr. Robbins echoed.

"Eliana, come over here." Her father's face was like stone.

Eliana walked up to the cavalcade, no bindings in place and her hair hanging in tangles down to her shoulders. She stood by her father's side. "Papa, you have it all wrong. A Ute attacked. Yiska saved me."

The group of men shifted their attention and scanned the area. A couple of them circled back and kept guard.

Warren Cates rode in a little closer. "That's not what it looked like from here. Looked like Wilcox was the Indian doing the attacking."

How dare he verbalize such an accusation? And in the presence of all these men, already gawking at her.

"Eliana, are you all right?" Mr. Mattheson asked.

Robbins narrowed his eyes, seething.

Eliana nodded toward Mr. Mattheson. Papa kept his eyes on her as he got off his horse. When he pulled her into the safety of his arms, she broke into tears.

Every bit the commander, Mr. Robbins pressed for details. "Where are the Utes now, Yiska? Why didn't you signal an alert?"

"It just happened. There was only one Ute, and I managed to trade Eliana's horse for her release. I'm confident the agreement satisfied him. I didn't want to risk an Indian war."

An odd twinge disturbed Eliana at the thought that her horse was more valuable to the Indian than she was. But what mattered was her value to Yiska. "Gentlemen. Stop pointing your guns at Yiska. He has done nothing wrong. . . or inappropriate. He handled the situation well."

"Do you care to share why we found you as we did just now?" Mr. Cates asked.

"*That* is none of your concern, Cates." Papa scolded.

"I beg to differ. Mr. Robbins, do you care to tell them, or shall I?" Mr. Cates sneered.

Chandler Robbins pulled a piece of paper from his pocket and held it up, along with a photograph of Eliana. "As we all can see, and evidenced by this photograph and the remarks on this paper, John Van Horn does not have a son. He has a daughter." Mr. Robbins narrowed his eyes at Papa then turned his attention to her. "Your name is Eli*ana*."

Papa looked askance at his comrade. "You knew?"

"I just learned of this a short time ago. I was about to discuss the matter with you when. . ."

The men grumbled. "Well looky here, now we got ourselves some female company," one said.

"Silence," Robbins commanded.

"Yes, sir. I'm sorry, sir." Eliana's face heated with shame.

Robbins spoke through clenched teeth. "Your apology will do nothing to help now. Having a female along puts me in a precarious position, miss, and all of us in jeopardy of harm. We have no choice but to pull out of here immediately and get across the border. We've come too far to safely turn back." Mr. Robbins's eyes flashed at Papa. "And then, Van Horn, I'll decide what to do about your *assistant*."

❧

Yiska kept his distance. Eliana rode double behind her father, and Yiska dared not speak to either of them until the storm blew over. As the team pulled forward, purple mountain vistas faded against the backdrop of looming sienna plateaus. The brilliant sunset of red and orange stretched across the early evening sky—a contrast to the dim mood of Chandler Robbins. The leader of the expedition had spoken little to anyone for the past few hours, casting a dismal shadow over all. At the border, Robbins and his surveyors set up their instruments and marked their first official point while several men stood guard, rifles in hand.

When they crossed into New Mexico territory, a feeling of familiarity came over Yiska. They were now in the land of the Diné, his mother's people—his people. Here on the Navajo reservation, the imminent danger of the Utes had passed. There was little threat of trouble with the Navajo here, and he would wear his headband to signify his kinship, though it would do little to ward off desperadoes. But he had a different force to reckon with now. Chandler Robbins. Yiska scouted ahead, all the while contemplating his and the Van Horns' fate.

He spotted the caravan headed toward him and trotted up to meet them. "Mr. Robbins, I found a place to spend the night in the shelter of some bluffs about a couple miles south."

Robbins rubbed the back of his neck. "How far is it to Aztec from there?"

"Twenty-five miles."

"All right. We'll spend the night up here. Lead the way."

Yiska shifted in his saddle. "Mr. Robbins. . .about today."

Robbins's lips drew into a line as straight as the Colorado–New Mexico border. "It's been a long day, Yiska. I'll speak with you and the Van Horns in the morning."

"Yes, sir. In the morning."

≈

The surveyors had already taken the measurements this morning, and the convoy of wagons and animals was all lined up and ready to go. But the entire cadre of workers sat in front of the campfire as Mr. Robbins paced back and forth.

Eliana bit her lower lip. Obviously, public humiliation was part of the punishment for her crimes.

"Yiska, let me get this straight. You knew about this arrangement all along?" Mr. Robbins asked.

"Yes, sir."

"And as the guide on this survey you didn't see the need to fill me in?"

"No, sir. I mean, sir, I wasn't concerned," Yiska said.

"And John, did you notify the GLO about the gender of your photography assistant?"

"It wasn't required on the application," Papa said.

"But you knew it was assumed that she—he—would be a male."

"That is typical, but I found no place to specify." Papa clamped down on his lower lip.

"Without my knowledge—or anyone else's for that

matter—that we had a female in our company, you put not only your daughter but all of us at risk." Robbins smacked his hat against his thigh. "Confound it. There shouldn't have been a need to know in the first place."

Mr. Mattheson cleared his throat and signaled Mr. Robbins with his pointing finger. "Chandler, I also knew."

"You're kidding me." Robbins laughed in disbelief. "No, I suppose you're not." He continued to pace. No one uttered a sound. "Is there anyone *else* who knew about this. . .other than Mr. Cates, who made a point of finding out?" Robbins's eyes narrowed at the man.

"I knew, Mr. Robbins," Cornelius Crawford said. "I promised not to tell. For her own protection. You wouldn't have wanted me to go back on my word. The good Lord wants us to be honest."

Mr. Robbins scratched his head and muttered. "Honest."

Eliana's face heated. She was next.

Mr. Robbins walked right up in front of her. "Miss Van Horn. Eliana—Eli. Very clever."

"Thank you, sir," she gulped.

Mr. Robbins crossed his arms. "No. Don't thank me. Just tell me. What on earth did you think you were doing?"

"I intended to assist my father with his photography on a survey expedition with the esteemed Chandler Robbins." She held her chin up. "I've been my father's right hand man. . ." A nervous guffaw escaped from her lips, but then she found her composure. "I've been helping him for years. He needed my help when he got the government contract to photograph the mines. He hired a man to assist him on this expedition. But he thought he had better prospects in the San Juans than on a desert survey. The disguise was for my protection."

"Are you quite through, Miss Van Horn?"

"Yes, sir." Eliana winced. "And please call me Eliana."

The creases in Robbins's forehead deepened. "Did my outfitter know about this scheme?"

Yiska spoke up. "I'm afraid so. Only recently."

Robbins threw his hands in the air. "Well, folks, looks like we're outnumbered. Unless anyone objects, *Eliana* will remain on the expedition."

"What about Wilcox?" Warren Cates protested.

"What *about* Wilcox?" one of the assistant surveyors asked. "He's been working twice as hard as you."

"He certainly has," another voice called out.

Eliana stood. "Indeed!" She defended him again. She covered her face in her hands and sat down, unable to look at Yiska.

Mr. Robbins let out a sharp whistle. "Settle down, or we're all going home. I'm paying you by the mile, not by the day. Time is money. And time is wasting." Robbins parked his foot on a boulder and leaned his elbow against his knee. "Now, although Eliana has proven that she is a capable member of this team—she even puts some of you to shame, I might add—I expect you all to treat her like a lady. No disrespect. Keep a proper distance. And let her do the work she came here to do."

He eyed Papa. "Does that sound fair?"

"Yes. Thank you. You won't regret it." Papa gnawed on his pipe.

"Eliana, is there anything else you'd like to add?" Mr. Robbins asked.

She offered a weak smile. "Well, I think we ought to be on our way."

Mr. Robbins shook his head and grinned. "The lady has spoken. Get ready to pull out."

Eliana's heart swelled. She was on an important survey expedition, not as Eli, but as Eliana Van Horn. A woman on an official government survey. Who'd have ever thought that possible?

seventeen

Aztec Ruins, New Mexico Territory

Yiska scanned the stone ruins from the outer edge of the encampment in Aztec, the remnants of pueblos left behind by an ancient tribe. As he fiddled with a dry blade of grass between his teeth he thought about the struggle to survive, only to have it all come to ruin—like it almost had for him yesterday. And to continue on, not knowing what still might crumble around him, and have the strength to stand. Must the motivations of one's heart always succumb to external elements? Would his?

Eliana's father ambled up to Yiska. "Impressive site. The masonry is astounding. It must have taken a long time to build."

"Some say it was built in the twelfth century, and here we stand admiring it." The ancient ones had disappeared with little to mark their existence but the sandstone rubble. What kind of legacy would Yiska leave? He had no home. No family. All he had were the words he wrote, which would leave little more of an impression on this world than Shadow's hoofprints in the sand.

Mr. Van Horn cleared his throat. "I'd like to speak with you about yesterday."

Yiska nodded and tossed the blade of grass to the ground. "All right."

"Tell me, what you were doing with my daughter by those pines?" Van Horn rocked back and forth on his heels. His mustache shaded the tight line of his mouth.

"I was, eh, buttoning her shirt." Yiska held up his hand. "She was shivering—in shock—and her shirt was undone."

Mr. Van Horn scowled. "Did the Indian do that?"

"I think she had, down at the river," Yiska said.

"Why was she alone?" Mr. Van Horn asked.

Yiska shrugged his shoulders. "She wasn't, not really. But she needed privacy. That's when the Ute found her."

"Regardless, it wasn't appropriate for you to. . .be so familiar with her." Mr. Van Horn glared.

Yiska looked back with a blank stare. Would Eliana's father rather that Yiska left her undone? It was no use reasoning with the man. He was rightfully upset.

Van Horn loosened his neckerchief and took a deep breath. "I hope you'll forgive me. I've been hard on you lately. My concern for Eliana. . . Well, I never did thank you." He extended his hand and offered Yiska a firm handshake. "You saved my daughter's life again and risked yours in the process."

"There's nothing to forgive. I'm glad I could help."

"Seems like you're always there when she needs you." Mr. Van Horn's mouth tightened. "I can see that you care about her."

Yiska looked down at his boots and contemplated his next words. Then he looked straight into her father's eyes. "She's a fine woman, Mr. Van Horn."

"You just remember what I said. If anything ever happens to me. . ." Mr. Van Horn wrinkled his brow. "I trust you, Yiska."

Why did this man keep talking like this?

"There you are." Eliana appeared, still dressed in men's clothing. But her hair hung down around her shoulders, and her face beamed like the sun. "Are you ready, Papa? I've got the cameras all set up."

"You didn't have to do that all by yourself," he said.

"I'm anxious to get started. Mr. Robbins and his crew are already at work, and everyone else is busy at their own tasks."

Yiska slid his hands into his back pockets. "Well, I guess we're slacking then."

"Good morning, Yiska." Eliana gave him a shy smile.

"Mornin'."

"Thank you again for. . ." She let out a little sigh. "I keep getting myself in trouble. But that's about to change. I'm feeling much more confident now."

Her father placed his arm around her shoulders. "Glad to hear it. Now let's take those pictures of the landscape, and maybe Yiska will help us explore the ruins."

&

Eliana stood in awe of the acres and acres of ancient dwellings laid out in a massive U-shaped configuration with hundreds of contiguous rooms. After taking an array of exterior photographs of the great Aztec Ruins, they met up with several of the others in the huge circular-walled structure in the center of the courtyard. Yiska remained behind, where she last saw him leaning against a wall of stone, pen and journal in hand.

Warren Cates's bravado bounced off the sandstone bricks in the open coliseum. "Remarkable. This place must have belonged to a wealthy leader. I could see myself living here if I were one of the Aztecs."

"Actually," Yiska said as he climbed through one of the openings, "this is a *kiva*, a ceremonial chamber like the smaller ones outside. These rectangles in the floor were baths, and this was a fire pit."

Mr. Cates's chest puffed out. "I read in one of the Natural History Museum publications that the Aztecs kept a continuous fire burning in hopes to bring back their Eternal King, Montezuma."

"That may be true, but the Navajo believe that these and other ruins like them belonged to the Anasazi—the ancient ones, or enemy ancestors."

Cates swiped his hand along his forehead, mocking the traditional Navajo headband that Yiska had worn since they entered Navajo land. "I suppose you can trust this uneducated half breed above esteemed archaeologists." He looked around at the group smugly.

"You do know then, Mr. Cates, that anthropologists are

now consulting with the Navajo and other tribes, like the Paiutes, to quantify their theories," Mr. Mattheson said.

"Well, it's neither here nor there."

"I beg to differ with you," Papa said. "We have much to learn from the past. About ourselves. The future."

How unusual for Papa to speak this way. He seldom looked back, but lately he had spent much time in conversation with Mr. Mattheson, reminiscing she hoped, discussing the reason Mr. Mattheson had left his calling. Papa positioned a camera and took a few photographs of the interior of the chamber.

"Mr. Cates, do you have any experience with cameras?" Eliana asked.

"As a matter of fact, I do. I've learned a little about photography during my tenure with the *Atlantic Monthly*."

Eliana eyed her father, who stood near Mr. Mattheson and Yiska. "Well then, perhaps you wouldn't mind taking a group photograph of the four of us. Then I'll be happy to take one of you, of course."

Mr. Cates acceded. "Ah, yes, of course."

&

Yiska and Eliana explored the many rooms of the immense stone fortress, talking as they climbed over piles of rubble, ancient steps, and dim passageways. Van Horn and Mattheson had returned to camp with Sampson, who had faithfully lugged their equipment to the site. The fact that her father entrusted Eliana to Yiska's care meant a great deal to him.

"Why do you think these dwellings were abandoned?" Eliana asked.

"One can only speculate. Drought maybe? Depleted resources. Maybe even war. There are other ruins similar to this. One is just ten miles south of here. And sixty-five miles farther, there's a much larger ruin in the Chaco Canyon," Yiska said.

"Larger than this?" she asked.

"Ten miles wide. The dwellings rise up five levels with

grand arches and ornamentation."

Eliana tilted her dimpled chin. "How do you know so much?"

"I've met a lot of people in my travels, and I read as much as I can. I wish I could take you there. You could take pictures and show them to the world. You'd become famous."

Eliana laughed. "And you would write all about it and become known to all as an expert journalist. You would no longer be the Anonymous Explorer, but the esteemed Yiska Wilcox."

He stood a little taller and suppressed a smile. "I do know this—the correspondent who writes about the Chaco Canyon ruins will make quite a name for himself. Mr. Robbins was good enough to give us time here while the animals rest today, so I guess we'll have to be content exploring the impressive Aztec Ruins." And perhaps to discover the unexplored territory of Eliana's heart.

They turned a corner and entered a long corridor of rooms connected by a passageway of successive doorways. Eliana grabbed Yiska's hand. "Come on, let's see." As they approached the doorway, she slipped her hand out of his, ran ahead, and ducked behind a wall.

Yiska caught up with the mischievous explorer, finding her with hands pressed against the wall behind her, taking in heavy breaths amidst intermittent giggles. He trapped her against the cool stones, one hand on either side of her, and tried to catch his breath. After a moment they both relaxed, but he didn't move his arms. Nor did she object. Yiska leaned toward Eliana and placed his mouth upon hers, the timeless moment blazing like the hot New Mexico sun.

He pulled away from her, his heart racing like a herd of wild horses. He forced himself to withdraw from her intense gaze. His eyes locked on a spot in the stonework behind her. "Fingerprints."

Eliana blinked. "What?"

"There are fingerprints of the builders in the mortar, right there." Yiska pointed his chin.

Eliana turned to look, still enclosed in the prison of his arms. He wasn't ready to release her just yet.

"Imagine, after all these years. Someone has left a permanent mark." Eliana turned back around, back still against the wall.

She tilted her head up, and Yiska admired the graceful arch of her neck. He stroked the smooth skin with a feather-light touch, following her gaze to the ceiling. "Those are original timbers, still in place after all this time." Leave it to him to spoil the mood, prompting her to slip down under his arm and make her escape.

Eliana skipped away, passing through a few doorways. Yiska followed at a slower pace. Let her play her game—he intended to win. But as she passed through the next doorway, Cates jumped into her way, blocking her path.

"Out of the way," Yiska commanded.

"I just want to have a word with the pretty lady." Cates feigned innocence. "What are you doing spending your time with a novice like him when you could enjoy this fine day with me?"

Yiska put his hand on his hatchet. "You don't know who you're up against."

"Don't threaten me, Wilcox," the weasel said.

"I'm not speaking about me. It's Miss Van Horn that you need to worry about."

Eliana turned back and flashed Yiska a smile. She put her hands on her hips. "Let us pass, Mr. Cates. We have work to do."

❧

After dusk Eliana and her father finished processing photographs from the day using their small portable darkroom under the shelter of their tent. Eliana opened the door flaps to let the remainder of the evening light in. "I almost forgot to mention, we found Anasazi fingerprints in a stone wall today."

"That's a remarkable find. It's unfortunate something like

that is too small to photograph," Papa said, wiping his hands on his canvas apron. "Harland found an ancient relic."

"I'll have to take a look when I'm done." Eliana went outside and sat on a stool at a worktable and wiped the dust from the equipment. "I'm so glad you allowed me to come on this expedition, Papa. I'm discovering so much about the world and myself." Foremost in her mind, the discovery she had made today about her feelings for Yiska. The warmth that spread from her toes all the way to her cheeks when he'd kissed her had taken her by surprise—and she hadn't even been blushing at the time. Was this what it was like to be in love?

She looked up and pushed the hair back from her face. "You seem to have enjoyed rekindling your friendship with Reverend Mattheson. I mean, Mr. Mattheson."

"*Reverend* Mattheson is correct. His faith has been tested, but he'll come around."

Eliana smiled. "I'm so glad to hear that." When she completed her task, she put the supplies away. "I think I'll go take a look at that old relic."

"Were you talking about me or my artifact?" Mr. Mattheson chuckled as he poked his head outside his tent door.

"There's the old fossil now." Papa grinned.

"Papa told me about your discovery." Eliana looked with interest at the small box he held.

Mr. Mattheson sat down at the table with Eliana, took an object out of a box, and held it up. She took a close look at what appeared to be a ladle. "How fascinating. The painting on it is beautiful. Do you think there is any significance to the design?"

"I'm no expert, but there may well be." Mr. Mattheson cocked his head and grinned. "That's quite an astute remark. Reminds me of my wife. Essie used to look beyond the obvious for the deeper meaning in things. She would have enjoyed knowing you." His eyes lingered on Eliana's face.

A moment later Mr. Mattheson stood abruptly and almost dropped the piece of pottery. Eliana wrapped her hands around his to steady his grip.

"Thank you," he said. "It would have been a shame if it had broken. Some things cannot be repaired." As he wrapped the piece in several layers of cloth and placed it in the box, Eliana had the distinct feeling that he was thinking of something— or someone—else.

She rose from her seat. "Papa, we haven't been keeping up on our evening Bible reading, and today is Sunday. Reverend Mattheson, perhaps you could read for us and share some of your insights."

"I don't know about that. It's been a long time," he said.

Eliana folded her hands and rested them on the table. "Please, it would mean so much to me."

A look of defeat crossed his face. "I'm not worthy. Never really was."

"Are any of us truly worthy to do what the Lord asks of us? You taught me that when I lost Josephine," Papa said.

"I remember. You weren't feeling up to the task of parenting alone. But you've done a splendid job, my friend." Reverend Mattheson smiled at Eliana.

"You said the Lord would equip me for the task, and He did. He'll do the same for you," Papa said.

Reverend Mattheson took Eliana's hand, "How can I complain? I'm ashamed I didn't initiate the idea myself, being the Lord's Day. God knows I need some nudging, and you were just the one to do so."

"She *has* been known to get her way," Papa chimed in. "And I've heard that our heavenly Father has a way of bringing us back around."

Eliana knew her father meant his own time in the wilderness as a young man, and his friend's role in bringing him back to the Lord. If not, what would have become of her?

Papa placed the Bible in front of his friend.

"That's Mama's Bible," Eliana said.

Reverend Mattheson wrinkled his brow and shook his head. "Then I'm definitely not worthy. But as you said, it's the Lord who equips us. Even this broken vessel."

"Good evenin'." Yiska sauntered up to the table. "I hope I'm not interrupting." He lowered a glance toward Eliana.

She offered him a small smile.

"You're right on time," Papa said. "That is, if you'd like to spend a few minutes with us while Reverend Mattheson reads from God's Word."

Yiska arched an eyebrow. "Reverend? I guess God equips anyone. No disrespect intended. I just never would have guessed."

"That's not to my credit. But coincidently, we were just talking about how it's our heavenly Father who makes us worthy, not ourselves."

Yiska sat down. "I do think I might be ready to hear what He has to say about that."

❧

The early morning sun greeted Eliana the following day, her heart full of praise. As they followed the river southwest, Mr. Robbins and his surveyors stopped for frequent measurements. This provided much opportunity to document the sublime landscape of sandstone arches, juniper-dotted deserts, and multicolored plateaus. Seeing Papa enjoying himself so much made her heart overflow with joy.

But the news Papa gave her that morning mattered most of all. Yiska had accepted Jesus as Creator and King. He had spoken with Papa and Reverend Mattheson at length about his questions after she had retreated to her tent and prayed.

He now understood the reality that Jesus was no mere man, but a divine being—God's only begotten, who was with His Father from the beginning of time and appeared to the world in the flesh. The Son had at last risen in Yiska's heart.

She couldn't wait to see Yiska, but he'd been detained with Mr. Robbins and his crew all morning.

Papa set up his camera overlooking a wondrous gorge layered with vivid earthen hues. The crisp, flattened tops of the plateaus contrasted with pointed mountaintops that were but a faded shadow of blue in the distance. On this side of the canyon, enormous sandstone rocks rose up around them, creating interesting places to explore.

Yiska walked up to the bluff and greeted Eliana. "Beautiful."

Upon hearing his voice, she turned around. "Yiska. It is a beautiful world. I thought my eyes had beheld all its loveliness in the San Juan Mountains, but here I see a new kind of beauty that I never even knew existed."

"That's exactly how I feel today."

Eliana continued to stand several feet away from him, though never feeling closer, simply admiring Yiska and what the Lord had done in his life. What He had done in her own, for she, too, was growing in faith every day. Some days flowed smoothly while others raged over rough waters, but through it all the current brought her closer to the Lord. She couldn't imagine that anything could spoil the joy she felt that moment.

Several feet ahead she spied Papa. He gradually backed away from his camera, gauging the perfect view, and stepped near a towering bank of rock.

A movement on the precipice above him caught Eliana's attention. She shaded her eyes just as a pile of rocks shifted.

A medium-sized boulder rolled off the crag and crashed down on Papa.

"Papa!" Eliana screamed as she flew to his side, Yiska right behind her. Reverend Mattheson dropped his sketch pad and hurried toward them.

Papa lay on the sandy ground, bleeding from a gash in his head. The boulder was in pieces near him, stained with blood.

"I'm right here, Papa." She cradled his head in her lap as tears poured down her face. "I love you, Papa."

Reverend Mattheson hovered over him, gripping her father's hand. Nothing else could be done.

A small stream of blood trickled from the corner of his mouth. Papa took a shuddering breath and spoke his last words. "Tell her."

eighteen

Sobs wracked Eliana's body as she leaned over Papa. *How could this happen?* A few moments ago he was enjoying his life, only to have it end in a flash.

Yiska's gentle hands helped Eliana to her feet. She fell into his embrace, releasing her grief and shock with a flood of tears.

After a moment, she turned to Reverend Mattheson, her hands still on Yiska's chest. "What did he mean? Tell me what?"

The man's eyes filled with compassion. "We can talk about it later, dear."

"No. I want to know now."

Yiska's warm hand stayed on her back. "Are you sure?"

A sob caught in her chest, and she tried to breathe. "Yes. I need to know."

Reverend Mattheson handed her a handkerchief. "Let's go over there and sit."

Yiska wrapped his arm around her waist and led her to the shade of ancient piñons, where she sat on a large boulder.

Reverend Mattheson covered the body of his longtime friend and joined them. "Robbins and the others need to know," he said to Yiska.

Yiska set his hand on Eliana's shoulder. "Will you be all right?"

"I'm in good hands. Thank you." She squeezed Yiska's hand and held it to her face before releasing it.

As Yiska walked away, he glanced back over his shoulder. Eliana's heart warmed to know his concern for her. She folded her trembling hands in her lap and bowed her head. She could find no words to pray but was thankful that her heavenly Father would hear the groaning of her heart.

"What did Papa want me to know?" She looked into Reverend Mattheson's ashen face.

"Perhaps it's best to wait until you are less upset," he said.

"I may already know." A look of surprise jolted his face. "Is it that he was not. . .my father?" Eliana clutched her stomach and took slow breaths.

"I don't understand," Reverend Mattheson said. "John said he never told you."

"He didn't. But when I was fourteen I found a letter you wrote to him, thanking him for adopting me. You asked him never to tell me about the circumstances of my birth—that my life would be ruined if I knew." Eliana turned away, the floodwaters threatening to flow once more.

"That was after I learned your mother died."

Eliana brushed away a fresh tear. "Papa was my father in every way that mattered. I didn't want anything to change. He was all I had."

Reverend Mattheson buried his face in his hands. He looked up and shook his head. "You've lived with this for all these years, dear girl." He wiped beads of perspiration from his forehead. "I never should have placed this burden on him. Nor should you have ever had to know."

"Burden? Is that what I am?"

Reverend Mattheson's face blanched. "No! You are not a burden. The only burden was my ill choice. I've carried around regret for my selfish decision ever since I made it." The man sobered. "I should have raised you myself. You were my wife's child."

Bile rose in Eliana's throat and she swallowed hard. She took a few deep breaths and walked over to Reverend Mattheson's side and sat with him on the large rock. "Don't say that. I was blessed to have Papa as my father. You gave me two amazing parents." A lump formed in her throat. "Though, if you had raised me, I'm sure you would have been a wonderful father as well."

"John Van Horn was a far better man than I will ever be. He took you into his arms as an infant and accepted you as his own without hesitation. He and Josephine loved every inch of you. She was a fine mother, as my Essie would have been."

Eliana sniffled, trying to restrain her tears. "There's more, isn't there? Tell me what happened."

Reverend Mattheson let out a deep breath and set his hat in his lap. "We were on our way west—Esther and I, your parents, and several other families. I was called to preach at the township we were headed to. The wagon train was attacked by Comanches. We managed to fight them off. But Essie. . ." He balled his hands into fists and turned his head aside, taking heavy breaths.

"You are not my. . ."

Reverend Mattheson's mouth formed into a grim line.

"Comanches." Eliana placed her fingers on her lips as tears pooled in her eyes, and she fought the nausea away. *I'm half Indian. Like Yiska.*

Reverend Mattheson stood and paced. "When we learned she was with child, I promised it didn't matter, that I'd accept the baby as my own. But when she died in her travail, I could barely face my life without her and could not comprehend how I would ever care for an infant." He looked at Eliana as if to gain her understanding.

"The infant who caused her death." Anger vied with compassion, creating a storm within her.

Reverend Mattheson rushed up to her. "No. You were an innocent babe. It was the Indian I blamed."

My father. But a small voice spoke to her heart. *Beloved, I am your Father.*

She looked up toward the bright sun and heaved a deep sigh. "Go on. Please."

"John and Josephine had always wanted children of their own. I placed you in their care and had them promise never to reveal the shame of your true parentage."

"Shame." Eliana swallowed. The Voice spoke again, quiet

and sure. *Those who look to the Son will not be ashamed. Look to me, daughter.*

"I continued my sojourn west and pastored that little church, but your parents settled in Missouri. I could only bring myself to visit a few times. You looked so much like your mother it hurt—so selfish of me." He gazed at Eliana for a moment with misty eyes. "Her hair was much lighter, and her eyes were blue. But your smiling eyes and that little dimple in your chin. . . You have her generous heart and feisty spirit as well."

Eliana let out a little whimper.

"The truth ate at me through the years. I was living a lie. It was I who bore the shame. I should have protected Essie. Kept my promise to her."

Eliana took a deep breath, trying to take it all in. "I'm sure you did everything you could."

Reverend Mattheson choked up. He turned away and looked into the distance, his hands plunged deep in his pockets. Before he turned around, he pulled out a handkerchief and blew his nose.

Eliana rose, compassion also rising within her for this hurting soul. "The last time I saw you, you baptized me."

"Yes, when you were twelve. It was my last baptism. After that, I realized what a hypocrite I was and left my days as a pastor behind me. Though it did little to appease my guilt."

"Reverend Mattheson." Eliana sighed. "I've always respected you. I don't hold your choice against you. You did well to place me where I could be best cared for—with a loving mother and father who longed for a child. But you gave me a heavenly Father as well, who has met my every need. And He will also meet yours, if you allow Him to."

Reverend Mattheson laughed and shook his head. "No wonder John called you Sunshine. Even now you are a shining light."

Eliana stepped toward her would-have-been father. "Would it help if I told you that I forgave you long ago? I wish I'd found a way to let you know. You and Papa carried an unnecessary burden on my account." Tears trickled down her face.

"Sweet child." He pulled her into his arms, and together they wept.

28

Yiska stood among the circle of men, hat in his hands, as Reverend Mattheson spoke at Eliana's father's grave.

"In John's last days, he had a chance to explore and photograph some marvelous sights, including the Aztec Ruins. The remarkable fortress of many rooms amazed him. But none of it compares to the wonders he is seeing in glory." He opened his Bible but did not read from the pages—he spoke the words from his heart. " 'In my Father's house are many mansions: if it were not so, I would have told you. I go to prepare a place for you. And if I go and prepare a place for you, I will come again, and receive you unto myself; that where I am, there ye may be also.' "

Yiska believed these words and rejoiced that this faith gave Eliana hope and courage, although her sadness was unmistakable.

When the service ended, Yiska enfolded her in his arms. If he could only absorb her pain the way his shirt soaked in her tears.

The somber caravan proceeded a few miles to Farming-town, at the confluence of the Animas, LaPlata, and San Juan rivers. Eliana now rode her father's mount.

Once they had set up camp, she retreated to her tent for a nap. Sometime later Yiska found her sitting alone by some low bushes.

"They call that Indian paintbrush." He pointed to the red flowers protruding from the sandy ground.

"Mmm. They're so pretty," Eliana said.

Yiska looked into her sleepy eyes, a little puffy from crying. "Would you like some company?"

"Please."

He sat on the ground. "Mr. Robbins tells me we'll stay all day tomorrow and leave the next morning."

"I'd prefer to keep going, but I know the animals need to rest," she said.

"He also needs to replenish supplies at the trading post and pick up the new sandstone marker for the four corners."

"I'm planning to complete this expedition. . .for Papa."

Yiska nodded. "I expected you would."

They sat in silence for several moments. Then Eliana looked at him with wide eyes. "I haven't told you about my conversation with Reverend Mattheson."

"You don't have to. Unless it would help."

Eliana nodded but said nothing until Yiska took her hand and gave it a gentle squeeze. "Reverend Mattheson's wife, Esther, was my real mother. He gave me over to the Van Horns when she died at my birth."

Yiska lifted his eyebrows. "Mattheson is your father?"

"That is what I believed. But, no. A Comanche warrior is." Her eyes shifted away.

Couldn't she bear to look at him? "Eliana. This must be a shock."

She bit her lip. "When I was fourteen years old, I discovered a letter from Reverend Mattheson to Papa revealing that I was adopted. I never told a soul."

Yiska retracted his hand. "Why didn't you tell anyone?"

Eliana looked back at him, her gaze intense. "I was ashamed. . .and frightened." She let out a deep sigh. "I didn't want to lose my Papa. I didn't understand the things the letter hinted at. I was foolish not to tell him. Something like that could have never changed our relationship. He will always be my father."

"What about your true heritage, Eliana?" Yiska asked.

"Essie Mattheson was also a Christian Jew. She led my mother to the Lord."

"And you are part Indian. Like me. Is that what you're ashamed of? Why you never told me?" If so, she would always be ashamed of him. The thought pierced him like a poison arrow.

Eliana looked at Yiska dismayed. "What do you mean? I'm not ashamed of you. Or myself. I didn't know who my true father was until today, or what had happened to my real mother. I'm disturbed by the horrific circumstances. I can't even think about it." She buried her face in her hands and wept.

"Eliana, forgive me. I never should have said that. I was afraid that this knowledge would make you despise me. . .and yourself. I couldn't bear that."

Eliana's tears flowed freely. "I could never despise you, Yiska. You are an honorable man." The corner of her mouth curved. "Even if you are a half breed." A whirlwind of laughter and tears mixed together. She leaned her chin on her clasped hands.

Yiska enclosed her hands in his and took in her sweet, precious face. "And now we know that the shadow catcher's daughter is also a half breed. A Comanche, you say?"

"Yes, and that's all I will ever know of him. But what is more important is that Papa loved me as his own, and I him."

Yiska look deeply into her eyes, her heart. "Your eternal heavenly Father knows all about *you*, and how you feel right now. At least, this is what I am learning."

"You're a good student." Eliana smiled.

Yiska pulled her close. "I've had an excellent teacher. She's quite the taskmaster."

&

After picking at her dinner, Eliana joined Yiska and the others who gathered on the porch of the trading post with their coffee. She sat to the side looking in the direction of the converging rivers, listening to their camaraderie and storytelling. Even so, she felt alone—until Chandler Robbins approached.

"Eliana, I'm sorry about your father. He was a good friend of mine back in the infantry. But now I'm in quite a quandary. You're no longer under his protection, and it's highly inappropriate for me to have a single woman in such a situation on this expedition. As you know, I've already gone against my better judgment to keep you with us, although you have proven yourself, and I don't regret it."

"Then let me stay."

"This goes beyond all protocol. I'm sorry, my hands are tied." Mr. Robbins looked at Reverend Mattheson, and his eyes narrowed. "Harland, you'll have to marry her."

Everyone quieted.

Reverend Mattheson's brow wrinkled. "Marry her? She's like a daughter to me."

"I know that. I mean you're a man of the cloth. You'll have to perform a marriage ceremony."

Eliana stood and stomped her boot. "I am not going to be forced into a marriage, Mr. Robbins. How could you suggest something so absurd?"

"Hold on now. Women have married for far less important reasons. If you can't find a suitable match among the men here, then you'll have to go back or wait here for us to return. And the latter is not advisable."

Eliana scanned the cadre of bachelors, all who averted their eyes. But there was one man that she'd consider as a husband—and he was looking right at her. Her face prickled with heat.

"If you won't marry, then I'll have to send you home. And there is only one person capable of seeing you back safely." Mr. Robbins looked directly at Yiska.

"No." Eliana planted her hands on her hips. "I cannot ask Yiska to give up his goals on my behalf."

"Eliana, I'll take you, if that's what you want," Yiska said.

She shook her head. "I don't want." *What I want is to. . .*

"Please calm down, Eliana," Mr. Robbins said. "Like the three rivers, it looks like you are faced with your own confluence of choices."

Mr. Robbins was right. The rivers flowed from various directions and she, too, must decide which way to go. She only wished someone else would make that decision for her.

੧

"Walk with me," Yiska said.

He took Eliana by the hand and headed toward the San Juan River, where he found a place for them to rest. The setting sun filled the horizon with vivid pinks, oranges, and reds. The colorful array reflected on the water, though nothing compared with Eliana's beautiful soul.

"It's so serene here. I wish I could capture it and put my thoughts to rest." Eliana faced Yiska. "I don't want to go back. I've made such progress with the photography on this trip. I want to see the project through. For my father. For me." She lowered her chin. "Is that selfish?"

Yiska shook his head. "Not at all. I understand. I have goals of my own to see through."

"And I would never want you to compromise them for me."

"I hope that won't be necessary." Yiska took some sand in his hand and let it sift through his fingers. "You know, Navajo healers create sandpaintings to help in times of grief and decision making. They draw a picture with different colored sands to reveal an answer for the troubled soul."

Eliana propped herself up with her arm. "Perhaps this Navajo can help me find a solution."

"I know you are seeking the path of God. Has He given you any insight?"

She shifted on the dry grass. "Some."

"Is marriage not an option?"

"Who would you want me to marry? Mr. Robbins? Warren Cates? Cornelius?" Eliana stifled a giggle.

Yiska did not laugh, and his stomach tightened. "I don't want you to marry any of them."

Her eyes widened. "Good, because I will only marry the one who loves me, the one whom I love."

The two sat in silence for several moments. Yiska drew a heart in the patch of sand in front of them. Eliana looked up at him, her hazel eyes dawning with understanding. She placed her hand over his and retraced the heart.

One heart.

Eliana whispered, "This is what the Lord has shown me, but I knew not how to ask."

"You don't need to ask. My heart already belongs to you, Eliana. I want to be your husband and journey through this life with you."

Crystal tears streamed down her cheeks. Yiska placed his hand behind her head and laced his fingers through her soft, full hair. The tender kisses that he placed on her lips mingled with her tears of joy and relief.

"We will marry tomorrow, if you'll have me. We can tell Mr. Robbins in the morning."

Eliana placed her hand on his face, and it warmed him down to his boots. "I love you, Yiska Wilcox."

"And I love you, Eliana. I think I always have."

Eliana glanced down at her shirt and trousers. "I suppose it's a good thing that I have my gingham dress along."

Yiska planted a kiss on her forehead. "You'll be lovely." Then he reached into his pocket and pulled out a piece of lace ribbon. "I've been meaning to give this to you for a long time now. Maybe you can wear it in your hair for our wedding."

"Yiska, it's beautiful." Eliana examined the lace. "This is from the mercantile in Del Norte. Don't tell me you've had it since then."

Yiska gave her a sheepish grin.

Eliana threw her arms around his neck. "Yiska Wilcox. Now *you're* blushing."

nineteen

How could a woman sleep the night before her wedding, the very day her father had died? But in the untamed southwest, deserts became sandstorms, reservoirs became raging rivers, iced peaks released avalanches, mountains buried treasure, and life went on. The rising sun greeted Eliana as she emerged from her tent and greeted the new day.

She yawned and stretched her arms high into the sky. Having slept some, she at last relinquished her struggle when early morning light brightened her tent. She sat outside and read Mama's Bible for over an hour, finally turning to the family record in the front pages. John Van Horn, father. Josephine Leman, mother. Eliana Esther Van Horn, daughter. Now she knew. Not only was Essie—Esther—Mama's best friend, but Eliana's middle name honored the mother who gave birth to her.

She turned the page. Deaths. She needed to enter Papa's death record. Her heart burned with sadness at the thought. The following page revealed a blank marriage certificate, and her pulse quickened. Reverend Mattheson would fill this in for her today when she became Mrs. Yiska Wilcox. Eliana Wilcox. She liked the sound of that.

"Miss Van Horn. Eliana." Warren Cates stared at her.

Eliana startled. "Really, Mr. Cates, must you always sneak up on me like that?"

"I have a solution to your dilemma," he said.

She closed the Bible in her lap. "Mr. Cates. . ."

"Hear me out. Come with me to Chaco Canyon and be my photographer. We will fully document the area and make a grand name for ourselves. Imagine the notoriety. You'll be published in the top scientific journals. You'll be the first woman photographer with that type of acclaim. Think of it!"

"I will have to decline, Mr. Cates. I've made other plans."
I would not marry a scorpion like you in a million years.

"What could be more important than an opportunity like this?"

"My wedding," she said.

"You've no need to marry. You can create your own renown. You and I will make a team. And then we'll see."

"I'm marrying for love, not for opportunity."

Mr. Cates' face creased with frustration. "Are you intending to marry that half breed?"

Eliana stood and crossed her arms. "I'm marrying Mr. Wilcox."

"For love?" Cates laughed. "What could he know about. . . Let me put it this way, Eliana. If you don't come with me, his short career will be over before it even begins. I will smear his name all over—" Cates grabbed Eliana by the arm.

Yiska, Mr. Robbins, and Reverend Mattheson walked up behind Cates. Yiska twisted the man's arm behind his back. "That'll be enough, Cates."

Mr. Robbins jabbed his finger in the man's chest. "Let me put it to *you* this way. You're off the expedition and going back the way you came. And if you dare make one disreputable remark about this fine correspondent, the *Atlantic Monthly* and every other magazine will have a full report from the government to discredit anything you write regarding any of the territories in these four corners, or anywhere else for that matter. Do I make myself clear?"

Warren Cates scowled and spit on the ground missing Yiska's boots. "Yes."

Mr. Robbins gave him a push. "Pack your gear and go."

Yiska wrapped his arm around Eliana, and Reverend Mattheson came alongside them. "I believe we have a wedding to plan."

⋱

Yiska bathed and readied himself for his wedding. He put on

clean trousers, a fresh shirt, and combed his hair—deciding not to wear his headband. Then he knelt down and prayed to his Maker to help him to fill the role of a husband in a way that would bring honor to God and give joy to his wife.

At the trading post Eliana waited for him with Reverend Mattheson, Chandler Robbins, and the rest of the survey team.

Yiska greeted her with a wide smile. "I've come to collect my bride." She had pinned the strand of lace in her hair. He took the end of it between his fingers and whispered in her ear, "You are beautiful."

A Navajo weave scarf adorned her gingham dress, and she had fastened a silver concha at the neck. She must have purchased them from the trading post.

Cornelius handed her a fist full of desert flowers—Indian paintbrush, larkspur, fiddlenecks, and others. "Every bride needs a bouquet."

"How thoughtful. Thank you, Cornelius." Eliana then eyed Yiska and pointed to the spot where her camera was all set up.

"Mr. Robbins has agreed to take a wedding photograph of us after the ceremony. That is, if you don't mind." Yiska recalled the day she had taken his picture and captured his heart forever.

Reverend Mattheson walked up to the two of them and placed a hand on each of their shoulders. "Are we ready?"

Eliana hesitated. "We have no rings."

He reached into his pocket and held two gold rings in the palm of his hand. "This is your father's wedding band. I thought you might need it." He smiled at Yiska.

Eliana looked at the smaller one. "And the other?"

"I've carried this with me for nearly twenty years. It belonged to my wife. . .your mother." Mattheson choked. "I'd be honored if you would wear it."

Eliana pressed her hand to her chest, and tears welled up. "The honor will be mine." She reached out and hugged him.

Yiska and Eliana led the procession down to the river's

edge, where they pledged their lives to one another. After they exchanged rings, Reverend Mattheson handed Eliana an earthen vessel that Yiska had obtained at the trading post. "It's a Navajo wedding vase," Yiska said.

She studied it with curiosity. "It has two spouts."

"The bride and groom each drink water from it to symbolize two souls drawing spiritual nourishment from a single source." His eyes penetrated hers. "Our source is Christ, the river of life. He is the sun in my shadows, the light that brightens the shadows of my past. And He has blessed me with you."

"And me with you." Eliana took a sip from the vase, her glistening eyes upon him. She handed it to Yiska, and he drank from the opposite spout.

Yiska gazed at her, memorizing the moment, the way he felt with the late afternoon sun shining down upon him. . . them.

Tears of joy streamed down her cheeks and trailed over her lips. Yiska brushed light kisses over her moist mouth, sealing his love for his bride.

❧

Eliana knew her face was as bright as the crimson sunrise when she exited her wedding tent with her husband the morning after they celebrated their holy matrimony. How wonderful it was to lie in Yiska's strong arms that night, reflecting on the joy of their marriage. But today was a new day, and the team would make the final leg of the journey toward Wilson's Peak.

The heat of the day as they rode through the desert would have been unbearable, if not for the light breeze coming off the San Juan River.

Yiska pointed to a huge, jagged rock formation protruding out of the sand several miles away. "There it is. Wilson's Peak. Some call it Shiprock, saying it looks like a clipper ship. But the Navajo called it *Tse` Bit' a i`,* 'rock with wings.'"

"I can see how it got its name." Eliana looked at the mysterious pinnacle and thought of how strange her life had become. Would they live in her house in Lake City? Could she keep the photography studio? Did Yiska want a family? "What else do you have in view, Yiska? I mean after the expedition. Will you continue to work for Mr. Whiley as a guide?" What would become of her if he was gone for many months?

"I plan to make a home for my wife. For my children. Mr. Whiley is thinking of opening a second store in Lake City. He might let me run it, and I could also write for one of the newspapers. I have some money saved, so I hope we might keep your house and your photography studio."

"Oh, Yiska. Your plans are wonderful. It sounds like you've given them much thought."

"That's what a man does."

"And a woman."

Yiska rode Shadow closer to her, leaned in, and planted a kiss on her lips.

When they arrived near Wilson's Peak in the late afternoon, the surveyors set up their equipment and spread out in a triangular formation at points surrounding the pinnacle. It took quite some time to complete their measurements and document the astronomical coordinates. Eliana set up a camera on its stand to photograph the massive rock and the landscape of low plateaus and interesting formations.

By nightfall the team had settled down and gathered around the campfire. Rich blues and reds cast a luminous glow in the cloudy evening sky, creating an eerie backdrop against the great winged rock. Eliana missed Papa. She could imagine him sitting there chewing on his empty pipe, gazing up at the brilliant colors.

Cornelius slapped his hat against his leg. "Take that!" He looked up, all eyes on him. "A sand spider."

"The Navajo believe that killing a sand spider can make one bald," Yiska said. He leaned over to Mr. Robbins as he pointed to Cornelius's balding skull. "He has killed too many sand spiders." Laughter echoed into the night.

"You know so much, why don't you tell us about that

fearsome rock over there." Cornelius nodded toward the silhouette of the pinnacle.

"All right," Yiska said. "A long time ago, the Diné were saved from their enemies after praying to their gods for deliverance. The ground rose, and they were transported into the east and lived on top of the rock. One day during a storm, while the men were away working the fields, lightning split off the trail, and only the sheer cliff remained. The women, children, and old men left on top starved. Their bodies are there to this day. It is forbidden to go there, so no one can stir up their ghosts or rob their corpses."

"That's a cheerful tale," Cornelius snickered.

Eliana hugged her coat around her and inched closer to Yiska. "Do you know any other Navajo legends?"

"There is another one of a large bird named Picking Up Feathers. He was the child of Diné gods, Sun and Changing Women. He lived on top of the peak and fed on human flesh. Each day he flew to Where the Mountain Went Out on Top to get men"—he leaned into Eliana's shoulder—"but never women. He now lives in the Sun's house."

"I'm glad to hear that. I wouldn't want him to come down and take you away from me so soon," she said.

Mr. Robbins stood and stretched. "All right, time to call it a night. Remember, we're more exposed out here, so we'll tighten our watch. And as you can tell, the temperature will continue to drop during the night."

Eliana smiled. She had Yiska to keep her warm.

Robbins continued, "We'll pull out at dawn and head north to Darling's Line to locate the four corners marker." He looked over at Yiska. "Oh, and thanks for the stories, Yiska. Let's hope they won't give us nightmares."

ಸ

Four Corners – July 10, 1875

The next afternoon Eliana marveled when they reached the Colorado–New Mexico border in such good time. She was excited to finally see the original marker that Ehud Darling set in 1868. Mr. Robbins and his crew would install a new monument in its place, a seven-foot pillar of hard sandstone, and Eliana was here to document the historical occasion. She set up her camera, this time with Yiska's assistance. She thought it best to begin instructing him on how to handle the equipment. She'd need his help for the many hundred miles that awaited them as they continued south to survey the boundary between the Arizona and New Mexico territories.

"Is this where you want it?" Yiska asked.

Eliana turned around and checked the position. "Perfect. Thank you." Beyond him she noticed Chandler Robbins talking to his assistant surveyors. He seemed disturbed, and his hands flailed in every direction as he spoke.

A few minutes later, Robbins called the team together to explain the situation. "The marker is in the wrong location. According to my modern instruments, Darling fell three miles east of the proper intersection. It looks like we have to go a little farther west."

The teams loaded up and went on, and Chandler Robbins at last located the coordinates of the 37th parallel and 109th meridian from Washington.

Eliana held her camera on the site as Yiska helped some of the men lower the marker three feet into the ground while others kept watch with their rifles. The marker was set exactly in the place where the four territories intersected. Perhaps someday they would become states in this wonderful, wild land.

As the sun displayed its vibrant colors, Mr. Robbins and the survey team headed out to set up camp. Yiska helped Eliana load her photography equipment onto Sampson. And then he took her by the hand and walked her up to the marker for a closer look.

"Mr. Robbins etched the exact coordinates here, and the name of each territory on the sides." Yiska pointed to each one. "Utah, Colorado, Arizona, New Mexico."

Eliana looked with interest at each side of the square column. She tilted her chin and suppressed a smile. "There's only one problem, husband."

Yiska placed his hand on his hat and squinted. "What is that, wife?"

"You must decide where to kiss me." Eliana circled around the tall stone. "Here, here, here, or here?"

"That's no problem at all. I will kiss you in each territory, here and everywhere else on our journey.

"And I will hold you to that promise, my love."

Under the canopy of an Indian paintbrush sky, Yiska kissed Eliana. Again. And again. And again. At that moment Eliana knew the memory of this day would remain engraved on her heart forever, the perfect reward for the shadow catcher's daughter.

Dear Reader,

The Shadow Catcher's Daughter is my debut novel, and what an adventure it has been! I hope you enjoyed traveling along with Eliana and Yiska on their romantic journey as much as I did. Though their story is fictitious, the actual 1875 survey of the Four Corners was real, so I decided to have my characters tag along. Using the latest technology at the time, surveyor Chandler Robbins set the boundary for the corners and discovered the earlier survey at Shiprock, NM, was incorrect. A recent controversy indicated that the monument may not have been correctly placed as measured from the Greenwich Prime Meridian. But prior to 1912, and at the time of the 1875 survey, coordinates were measured from the Washington Meridian (about 3 miles difference). This is inconsequential, however, because the border between the states, as determined in the Robbins's survey, was accepted as the legal boundary. Today's monument is exactly where the state lines intersect.

When reading about Chandler Robbins I discovered that he served with photographer James F. Ryder in Ohio's 86th Infantry during the Civil War. Ryder is famed for capturing the war with his camera; thus I decided to make him John Van Horn's mentor, which in turn connected the three men as old wartime companions. Ryder stated once that what he saw through the lens of the camera was "faithfully reported, exact, and without blemish." That is how our heavenly Father sees his children. I do hope you believe how precious you are to Him.

I have a few other "real" characters like Mr. Wilson and Mr. Snowden in my story, but my favorite secondary character is Reverend George Darley. He was known as "missionary to the San Juans" and really did preach in saloons! He and his brother built the very first church on Colorado's western slope in 1876. For more information about the research involved in this novel and to learn more about George Darley's extraordinary adventures, please visit me online at carlagade.com.

I hope you will enjoy the next two books in the Love in Four Corners series by my own fabulous mentors—*Pride's Fall* by Darlene Franklin and *Almost Arizona* by Susan Page Davis. We are pleased that this series is releasing in the year that Arizona and New Mexico are enjoying the first centennial of their statehood.

Love & Blessings,
Carla Olson Gade